The Mighty Six-Ninety (690)

The Mighty Six-Ninety (690)

A Novel By

Alexander Hamilton Cherin

ISBN: 979-8-9894672-0-4

First Edition, 2024

Printed in the United States of America

Inspired by Actual Events

LAST DAY OF THE CONTEST

Chapter I

Last Day of the Contest

Friday, July 3, 1981
East Los Angeles, CA

At approximately 7:45 on the morning of July 3, 1981, the entirety of Chavez Ravine stood eerily silent. Three weeks into the Major League Baseball strike, and with the larger wake of white flight from the East Los Angeles suburb in which it sat still palpable, what had become the permanent home of Dodger Stadium (and about fifteen hundred Angelenos to boot) was now virtually lifeless. No parking attendants, no vendors. Certainly not the incessant, low-grade hum or noise that only a game day could bring. That is, of course, with the notable exception of the staccato footsteps rapidly approaching like a groundswell from what seemed to be the lower part of Lot F. It was, after all, the nearest parking lot from the Sunset Boulevard entrance and not so coincidentally, the only one open on non-game-day mornings.

Four people, strangers to one another, carrying shovels of varying sizes, emerged from the silence of the morning, sprinting with particular purpose toward a visible opening in the outfield wall, which was the only thing separating the parking lot from the confines of the playing field. A corrugated metal door with meshed fencing measuring about five feet on top and slightly frayed from the droves of eager fans without tickets trying to catch a glimpse (at least when the season was being played) was slightly (and intentionally left) ajar.

The four strangers, who were now making their collective way toward the opening into the stadium, had seemingly arrived just moments before daybreak, in unison within a minute or so of each other. One, in a beige 1977 AMC Hornet that was abruptly parked by one of the few palm trees left alive in the stadium parking lot; one on a nondescript and well-worn crimson 1973 Honda that had clearly seen better days; and two by foot.

As the collective cadence of their footsteps grew and as they were within throwing distance of the open gate, they all had one thing in common—they were laser-focused. As if on cue, a mist began to thicken around the undulating parking lot and the surrounding landscaping. It provided a dramatic backdrop to the four as they reached the gate and began to enter. Such a mist was a rarity at this time of year, as usual mornings were shrouded in heat and haze. The coolness belied the intensity of the strangers' focus.

As they ran across the chipped transition between the parking lot and stadium and up the concrete foot ramp into the centerfield veranda, they noticed even more strangers. But these folks were not carrying shovels. They looked corporate and official, and the four, who had now confirmed they were in the right place, blew them off with a deliberate indifference and continued to run.

Like a herd of savannah beasts being studied from afar, they continued—hurriedly—along the concourse toward what appeared to be an opening down onto the field. They were keenly unaware of who among them would be the one to find it.

A week of anticipation had been quite enough for most of them.

They funneled, lemming-like, onto the grassy field and continued to run toward the well-manicured, light brown dirt of the infield, shovels still at the ready. In the late 1970s, the grounds crew of the Los Angeles Dodgers were world-renowned for their attention to detail and what was considered in the baseball world to be a bit of creativity with patterns and spacing that would be considered sacrilege to baseball purists. The pristine condition of the dirt was in exceptional form on this particular early July morning. On any other morning, the four would have been stopped at the gate, politely asked to return to their seats, or, in more egregious situations, removed from the stadium altogether. But today, both stadium security guards and a handful of others—the observers without shovels—were milling about in the lower sections of the stadium, watching with a hardened interest the goings-on in front of them.

As the four strangers began to disperse to various areas of the infield like a well-coached little league team being summoned to the field from the dugout at the direction of their coach, the sharp cadence of metal shovels hitting dirt began to resonate, one after another, after another. One began digging just to the left of where third base should have been, one dug near second, and the others focused on home plate. There were slight glances at each other's handiwork—and progress—as they focused on deliberate and heavy digs into the soil. The pace grew more rapid as the grey palate of early morning fog and mist continued to drift in. One of the four, a tall, battered-by-life male seemingly in his thirties, began to sweat. The only woman in the bunch, who seemed to cough with every dig she dug, partly out of anxiousness and partly from fatigue, was showing signs of tiring. Another, not looking much older than a teen, dug as fast as he could. And the fourth, an older man who, by all appearances, did not seem to fit in, stood almost defeated, not knowing how to help.

And just as quickly as they had begun, the crisp and sudden sound of metal hitting metal—loud enough to be heard throughout the stadium and parking lot—stopped them all abruptly, mid-motion. Standing erect and at attention, they stared at each other in a sort of collective inertia. What appeared to be the surface of a sterling silver box—like the kind you would find in a bank safety deposit vault—had been unearthed. A smile began to grow, albeit cautiously, on the one whose shovel had been just a bit luckier than the others. The rest of them stopped, graciously resigned to their defeat and began to slowly walk back toward the parking lot they had emerged from minutes earlier. ⋆

Chapter 2

Sunday, June 28, 1981
Baja del Sur, Mexico

Ernesto Hernandez had received the call only forty-five minutes earlier, but he was already pushing open the side-hinged gate allowing access to the uneven gravel road situated just north of the highway turnoff for Avenida Playa del Rosarito and two miles south, as the crow flies, of the immigration processing center at the international border. His diligence and time management skills were not lost on him. As the gate swung just wide enough to allow him through, he quickly rushed out of the brisk, summer morning air (which by local standards was colder than normal) and into the temporary warmth of his white 1968 Chevy truck, restarted the engine, and pulled the gearshift loudly into drive. He glanced upward toward the top of the dirt hill he was about to climb and saw the first hint of morning sun spilling over the Baja skyline.

Pemex—the Mexico City–based conglomerate that dabbled in oil, minerals, and in some instances, political corruption—had once owned and operated the road, as well as the looming transmission tower that stood atop the hill like a stoic steel monolith on what was, to date, the highest point of the Baja Peninsula. It was a well-regarded and easily discernible landmark for the locals and known to the gringo travelers looking for safe backways and shortcuts around Tijuana.

That all changed ten months ago, however, when Ernesto's employer sold the road and the transmission tower that came with it (package deal) to a new company based in San Diego. They had apparently made plans to use the tower to host a "border blaster" radio station specializing in pop music for their more economically privileged neighbors to the north.

Ernesto had been involved in making the initial structural changes to the tower that were necessary to accommodate the new fifty-thousand-watt platform that would now be needed to carry the radio waves up through the Baja peninsula into the metropolitan San Diego area and then continue east and north, off to the Imperial Valley as well as into suburban Los Angeles. He had also spent a significant amount of time installing new cabling, a borrowed electrical "switchboard" from a related Pemex venture in Ciudad Juarez (which was now defunct for some reason), and thirty gallons of paint to mute the more obvious rust patches.

Returning twice since those times for only slight repairs (this morning in June being the third), Ernesto tried to quell what was now, upon reminiscence, a bit of anger. Towers like this one throughout Baja (although not as high nor as prominent) had started to pivot—both literally and figuratively—over the last few years from pointing south (to *la gente*, he thought) to pointing north toward los Estados Unidos. It signified more than a physical shift in direction to Ernesto, but he was able to summon a bit of cognitive dissonance and press on. He had a job to do for now, and for now, that was enough.

The tower was originally constructed seventeen years earlier as a simple ten-thousand-watt tower to facilitate the flow of *Banda* and *Norteña* music to Tijuana locals. Still it could be heard sometimes late at night, without competing radio traffic as far away as San Felipe. In the interim years, the tower's broadcast platform had changed hands three more times—twice to competing Mexican companies based in Acapulco and Guadalajara, respectively, and most recently to the gringo radio station just across the border in San Diego operating as the Mighty 690, a name Ernesto did not quite understand. Or care about. He had no reason to. But his bosses did.

As his truck tires slowed and pebbles from the finely crushed gravel could no longer be heard pinging the inside frame of the wheel well, he parked the vehicle at the apex of the hill, right at the foot of the giant tower, and started to lumber out of the cab. What had only moments ago been faint glimpses of sunshine now gave way to shining slivers of iridescent orange amplified against the vast sea of tin roofs lying below. Tin roofs that in any other country would be called shanties, but in Baja were far too commonplace to be called something so pejorative.

Ernesto walked toward the tower as he clamped his leather tool belt tightly to his waist. Small dust clouds, created by a combination of his old work boots and years of overindulgence in his wife's flautas, began to rise and then disappear quietly into the crisp morning air. He looked up, tipped his ball cap, and assessed the situation.

His boss—the well-known but not particularly well-liked Juan Benitez Ovalle (whom his workers simply called *el jefe* out of convenience, not respect), had told him that the main "switchboard" (the one that had been borrowed from Ciudad Juarez), had once again shorted out and abruptly stopped the station's transmission into the States. Several calls had apparently been received from angry teenagers and morning drive-time audiences.

Unbeknownst to Ernesto, as he began to ascend the narrow metal ladder to set about on his repairs, was that the radio landscape of Southern California in the summer of 1981—much like the physical nature of the towers he worked on—was in frenetic transition. Once dominated by big companies that would hire big personalities to spin big records that their sponsors and corporate friends would tell them to, local radio in the 1970s had ushered in a more parochial flavor. Los Angeles FM stations like KRUZ and KLAA would play rock, while splinter stations would flirt with more progressive fare like punk, Latin, and even Reggae. By 1981, as the suits at the company that had just launched the Mighty 690 learned, there was clearly room and need for a resurgence, of sorts, of pop music. But that resurgence had been relegated to AM. FM was simply too expensive, as Ernesto's bosses, including *el jefe*, had been told. The cultural, political, and entertainment fates had created a unique cultural intersection between blue-collar AM and the more stylized and bourgeois FM fare. And that intersection is where a tired but determined Ernesto Hernandez found himself on this nondescript morning on the shallow and gray outskirts of Baja California, Mexico.

But he reminded himself again that he had a job to do. Five minutes of dead airtime, especially to listeners of a fledgling pop AM station in this era, was reason enough to turn the dial.

No loyalties, no regrets. And the fact that the station was on the precipice of launching a radio contest added to the pressure.

As Ernesto reached the second level of the tower, the rusted iron housing of the "switchboard" seemed at first glance to be intact. He was disappointed, as this meant the problem, if any, would require him to climb the additional series of narrower switchback ladders even higher until he found whatever it was he needed to fix. And with that, he pulled the first ladder down to shoulder height and put his right foot on the bottom rung with a grunt and a prayer. He ascended to the third and then the fourth segment of the dilapidated ladder that looked more like something from his *tio*'s junkyard off the old road in Rosarito that catered to broken-down tourists. At about the halfway point, just around the portion of the tower that became noticeably and annoyingly narrow—at least for those who had to climb it—he saw the splayed wire as if it were some gutted, sinewy fish made up of copper and metal tubing. It wasn't the "switchboard," after all.

He gazed down at his tool belt and went to work. Any hopeful thoughts he had of returning to a still-warm bed were now long gone. And as interesting and important as the history of the station for which he worked and the radio climate of the 1980s may have seemed to his bosses, at this particular moment, the whole of the broadcast lay on the shoulders of a thirty-nine-year-old Ensenada resident who would much rather have been sleeping in.

But Ernesto began to ply his trade proudly. Twenty-two minutes to the second after he had started, the last edge joint had been welded to resurrect the tower's functionality, and in an instant, the transmission began to flow.

Although not aware of the exact second the station began to transmit music again, as the thousands of Americans to his north stopped hitting the sides of their wooden Kenmore radios or stopped frenetically twisting the silver tuning dials to home in on its signal, the sound of Laura Brannigan, mid-chorus, could be heard loud and clear.

Both proud and fatigued, Ernesto descended the tower, climbed back into the warm confines of his truck, and headed down the hill, back toward Ensenada, and into what hopefully was the last thirty minutes of an otherwise good night's sleep. ⋆

Chapter 3

September 9, 1980
Orange County, California
9:20 a.m.

The Buena Park branch of Great West Savings and Loan, near the southwest intersection of Warner Avenue and Harbor Boulevard, had seen better days. Nestled carefully between the newly opened "Chuck's Chicken Shack" and the "OC Skate and Surf" shop (which sold surfboard wax, terry cloth shirts, and two-tone OP shorts no less than fourteen miles from the nearest surf break to the south in Huntington Beach), the bank had just opened, and the smell of coffee from the single copper-tinged pot in the break room was making its presence well known. As enticing as the aroma was, signaling the hope of a fresh new day, the faded beige paint on the exterior of the building, situated squarely on the least-trafficked corner pad of the mini-mall, quickly dispelled any such transitory optimism.

Sally Lang had been a teller at the bank for seven years, almost to the day, and her modicum of interest in bank telling as a career had long ago subsided, as had her once-long brown hair, which gave way to a more palatable bob cut (to meet corporate expectations). Her singular focus was, and really had always been, on raising her nine-year-old son, Peter. Without a father, she was determined to make sure he would not carry the resentment of that fact too far along in his life.

And perhaps that is why, on that Tuesday in the fall of 1980, months before a radio station contest would be her only hope of redemption, and when Peter had just started the school year as a middle-of-the-pack fourth grader, she intentionally shorted the nightly cash count at the Great West S&L by $250, which she placed in the left front pocket of her Laura Ashley hand-me-down pantsuit.

Coincidentally, the amount was just enough to cover the gap caused by her need to also selfishly pay the car repair bill that week, but not enough to elicit the kind of fear and panic she had initially anticipated. After all, the Great West accounting protocols loophole was neither her fault nor that hard to exploit. Jeff Stoll, after all, was the branch manager who should have noticed and done something about it but didn't. Jeff was otherwise preoccupied, as he had a consistent affinity for wanting to get home early enough on weekdays—almost seconds after the bank's 5:00 p.m. closing—to quietly screw open the ever-dwindling bottle of Old Grandad on his bookshelf and be comfortably asleep (passed out) just as *Mannix* was ending. That way, the words of his wife of twenty-two years would not be so coherent (or caustic).

Sally had often rationalized that THEY, after all, had made a choice not to have tellers review other tellers' cash tallies after the tellers had rolled their carts into the back vault room, leaving open the very real possibility that someone motivated by filling a shortfall in the monthly budget could do so. The starting point for the nightly cash count was skewed—or could be skewed. And that is what Sally had done. And more than once.

As today was a Tuesday in September, the bank was slow. Between customers, Sally actually started to count, in her head, how much she had taken over the course of the last eight months. By her rough math, it was just shy of $9,000, and that was the type of cash (as Mrs. Kinkella highlighted by pointing out the sweat on Sally's forehead mid-transaction) that Sally could never pay back, at least for the foreseeable future.

"You doing okay, Sally?" asked Mrs. Kinkella, a regular customer who took out two tens and three fives for her grandchildren every week.

"I'm fine," she said, convincing no one.

Mrs. Kinkella obliged what she knew to be a courteous misrepresentation, but she appreciated the pleasantry nonetheless. Exchanges like this were not uncommon for Sally, but she hated them. Inauthentic and compulsory, she thought to herself. Hiding her ongoing embezzlement was the source of her concern, but she used the feigned politeness as a nice surrogate.

Quite frankly, she was perpetually occupied with the thought of how she would or wouldn't cover her tracks and pay the money back before Jeff, the *Mannix*-watching manager, would either call for a routine audit or catch her in the act outright. It kept her up at night, but then again, so did the thought of having to move away from Southern California with Peter and back to her parents in Ames, Iowa (or worse yet, a suburb of Ames), hat in hand and pride in check. It had been a rough go of it since moving here (some moments, in fact, were downright traumatic), but she had done her best in the last few years specifically to deal with that and wanted to stay put.

She was, by all accounts, stuck.

Just as Mrs. Kinkella finished her weekly ritual and was headed out the door toward Harbor Boulevard to disappear into the faceless, suburban Orange County autumn, Jeff made his presence known with a smile and an unwelcome touch on the shoulder.

"Sally, can you help Donna with the vault count this afternoon after she's off the floor?" He directed more than he asked.

She smiled slowly and nodded affirmatively.

Sally was secretly happy, as her days to do the count were Wednesdays and Thursdays, and this being a Tuesday meant, in a crude way, another $250 extra that was unforeseen. She was long over feeling guilty. She was now in the phase of acceptance. She was not proud of what she had done, but at the risk of buying wholesale into a cliché, she would do anything to give Peter the normalcy she had never known as a child and certainly not as a single, poor woman in early 1980s Southern California.

As her shift ended and she accompanied Donna to the vault, the usual industrial gray Panasonic radio was faintly but expectedly playing in the background. At that moment, Juice Newton's "Queen of Hearts" was playing on the Mighty 690—a default pop station for most of the employees in the bank. Self-aware and confident enough to realize that pop music was just fine for her, Sally and the other tellers gravitated toward the Mighty 690 and their consistent airplay of Top 40 music. It provided a degree of routine and familiarity that they longed for, and the overdose of melancholy and soap opera–like storylines in the lyrics was oddly satisfying. Something about the earthy quality of the AM bandwidth—static and all—appealed to the tellers, who ranged in age from twenty-nine to fifty-three. And in their shared listening, they found a sort of contentment.

Juice Newton's new hit was the exact sort of contentment that Sally and Donna needed to push through the final forty-five minutes of their shifts. The sound of the bulky corrugated tin carts with lopsided wheels echoed in the narrow hallway separating the bank lobby from the vault room. Faded brown doors that served as entryways to tiny, unimpressive offices lined the hallway. Sally and Donna continued to roll their carts all the way down the hall and to the last door on the right. Fumbling for his keys, Jeff (who would routinely accompany his tellers to the back during the cash count) opened the vault door for the two of them, motioned them in like a second-rate doorman in a Manhattan apartment building, and shut the door, leaving them to their business. Donna made no eye contact nor commented on the music coming from the radio, as she sometimes did to break the ice with Sally, whom she did not care for much socially since she was a single mother; Donna was too "Christian" and too condescending to approve of that lifestyle choice. Sally was glad and began to count before Donna could start talking. While she was slipping every fourth twenty-dollar bill into her clothing, neither Donna nor Jeff (nor anyone else for that matter) was any the wiser.

As she hid the fifth twenty-dollar bill and reminded herself, using her best math on the fly, that it would be enough to roughly cover the shortfall in her insurance, grocery run, and tutoring for Peter for the week, she stopped. Lifting her head in almost a conciliatory gesture, Sally grinned at Donna as if to ease the awkward silence.

"I love this song." ⋆

Chapter 4

December 12, 1970
Wilmington, California

Although Lions Drag Strip in Wilmington, California—a small pocket of single-family homes and old Croatian American eateries punctuated against the backdrop of the large cranes and terminal equipment at the Port of Los Angeles—had made a legitimate reputation for itself, it wasn't until Evel Knievel came to the track in December 1970 to jump thirteen cars that it really placed itself squarely on the map

Average race nights at Lions drew about three hundred (maybe four hundred if it was a school fundraiser or tribute night), but by any metric, this night was palpably different. Evel Knievel gained popularity in the late 1960s and 1970s daredevil culture—through media like the *Wide World of Sports*. His billed performance at Lions Drag Strip (which had actually printed and posted bills along Main Street, Pacific Coast Highway, and Avenue A for at least two months in advance) had piqued the collective interest of this small LA suburb. By 6:00 p.m. (thirty minutes before the first drag race prelim), there were at least five hundred people, and the beer line was only getting longer.

Most of the area's cool kids and younger adults who hadn't quite shed their love for motor sports, the absurd, or both were all there that night, soaking in the harbor air. All there to see Evel and maybe a buddy or two during the fourteen races scheduled around the main event. Cross sections of longhaired and blue-collar working men from Wilmington proper as well as nearby places like Carson, Long Beach, Lakewood, and even a smattering of rich kids from Palos Verdes, had all come to watch. Among the swath of denim jackets and smoke from freshly and skillfully rolled joints was Danny Baker. Nineteen years old and living at home with his mother, Penny (and Penny's longest boyfriend by six months easily), Danny worked ten hours a week at the Belmont Station auto repair shop and made just under four bucks an hour. Sometimes, he would get tips (about five bucks total) if a brake job got done before expected. These were numbers, all of them, that Danny could recite by rote.

But what he hadn't figured out yet was what he was going to do after the shop had a new owner. That was happening at the end of the month as the current owner, Arturo, an immigrant from Jalisco, was returning to his family to take over their farm and had sold the pumps, the gas rights, and the three vending machines to an Iranian family that had a penchant for the Shah and American ice cream. But they had already told Arturo that "family only" would be working there. And that did not include Arturo. Or Danny.

He was at a loss with that development, coupled with the fact that college was not even on the horizon of possibilities. But he didn't want to think about such serious matters tonight. He was there to see the daredevil himself—and to meet Brandon, his co-worker and former co-student through the tenth grade, at least when Brandon dropped out. They usually met by the food truck in the east corner of the lot. It was the least crowded, and the guy would throw on extra cheese at no cost if you asked him. They would spend their nights watching the races—betting a quarter on each.

However, despite the quarters he won from Brandon and the extra cheese, Danny was growing a bit tired of Saturday nights at Lions. But it was the closest thing he had to remembering the good times in his childhood. His dad had taken him here as a kid, and he had a particular fondness for it.

"Danny!" He heard Brandon call from behind him. Without having to turn around, he put his fist in the air as if to acknowledge his friend and signal that yes, once again, here is where the two prodigal children of the neighborhood, upstanding in every regard, chose to spend their Saturday night—again.

“Dude, I can’t fucking believe that, of all the places, he is going to jump here!” As if to simultaneously herald the iconic importance of Evel Knievel being at that drag strip and subtly diminish Wilmington’s stature.

“Why not here?” Danny thought to himself but didn’t utter a word.

Just as his mind loosened from the joint he had smoked an hour ago, the smell in the night air changed abruptly. What was earlier detectable as the innocent blend of marijuana smoke and car exhaust, now the air had given way to an intoxicating mixture of bunker fuel from the container vessel that had just docked at berth 54 and the ethanol emanating from the engines lining up at the start line of what was the first of six motorcycle races that night. While most were excited by the lights and sounds, it was that smell that captured Danny’s thoughts.

Lions was typically exclusive to auto racing. But the stunt involving Evel Knievel, which would occur between the third and fourth races, needed an additional draw. Pulling out all the stops, Lions—for tonight only—would deviate from custom and host motorcycles. In the world of gearheads and auto fanatics, motorcycles were gaining cultural popularity, and the old guard hated it. But those with a little bit less gray hair—they loved it.

The strip at Lions was a place where kids from blue-collar homes in blue-collar neighborhoods could race the fruits of their creative efforts throughout the week on fabricated open-wheel cars, homemade paint jobs, and adolescent arrogance. In the 1970s, as the kids in the neighborhood grew up, so did their tastes and interests. Dirt bike racing had taken center stage, and they would travel up the 15 Freeway to places like Victorville and Barstow to watch men slide their bikes sideways through the turns of ovals no bigger than high school running tracks. The Ogden family, who had owned Lions for more than a decade, noticed. So much so that Phil Ogden (no more than twenty-two at the time) convinced his father and the Wilmington City Council—in that order—to lay down dirt and make its own oval track for motorcycle racing.

When Danny saw the oval track that night—crumbled and crushed earth spread evenly—he knew he was hooked. As the remainder of the crowd ogled with hooked gazes on the man in the white jumpsuit with a Southern Cross pattern sewn across the front, Danny was drawn to the sideshow of motorcycles racing perpetually around an oval track.

And for only the second time in his life, he knew what he was meant to do. He would race motorcycles for a living. What that "living" looked like was irrelevant to him. Most stayed for Evel's jump that night, but Danny left after the third dirt bike race. He had seen enough to gain certainty. ⋆

Chapter 5

September 25, 1980
East Los Angeles, California

Despite an otherwise steel-trap mind, Augie Kloptman (born Augustus Abraham Kloptman on March 3, 1931, in Belarus, but now known by his more colloquial name) could never quite memorize the six digits tattooed onto his forearm in dark blue ink no matter how hard he tried. Just after he had moved to East Los Angeles in the mid-1960s, he had been able to recite five of the six, but never all of them. Perhaps it was a gift. The son of a Jewish garment manufacturer from Poland and his seamstress wife, Augie had entered the Bergen-Belsen camp with six family relatives (including his mother and father) and was only able to count two (which did not include his mother and father) by the time the camp was liberated by infantrymen in faded khakis on a bright day in April 1945.

Only fourteen, orphaned, alone, and scared, he left to navigate the countryside when the gates had opened before finding distant cousins near Gdańsk. Augie had been eternally grateful every day of his life since. Never more so, however, than the day he boarded the Red Star liner headed from Antwerp to New York and into a new life.

Processed through Ellis Island in just under an hour, he had one canvas bag, an extra pair of glasses, and nothing else as he walked north on Lexington Avenue to the doorstep of distant cousins. Raised by his mother's family for the next seven years, he was provided technical schooling and peripheral vestiges of love. When he turned fifteen, Augie went to work straight away. Under the tutelage of some neighborhood folks, he learned a trade and spent his days toiling in the shipyards of Brooklyn, working on commercial vessels mostly. He made friends—most of whom would gather Sunday evenings around 6:00 p.m. at the Jewish Community Center on Bayside Avenue to play bridge and pinochle. By twenty-five, he had managed (despite his background) to cobble together the basic ingredients of the American Dream.

But by twenty-six, he was getting older—as tends to happen—and lonely. The bridge games gave way to wedding parties and dances for married couples. So he set out to join them.

By the time Augie married Esther in the summer of 1957, he had forgotten the faces he saw in the camps. He was focused now on this wonderful new postwar American experiment, which promised him a better life and opportunity, regardless of the digits on his arm and the accent in his speech. And by the time the shipyards had all but shut down, the congregation of Temple Beth Am in Crown Heights, Brooklyn, had provided him with a job sweeping up after services (and b'nai mitzvahs of native-born and entitled American Jews, as he thought of them), and he didn't need or want for much else.

The janitorial job provided a simplicity and structure that his childhood had not accommodated. And he reveled in the mundane simplicity of it all. The faded elegance of the temple halls was enough for him, and Esther (whom he met at a Passover social event) was a good cook. She could not provide children for him, but after what he had been through and witnessed, he was not convinced that this world was a good place for children. He was content.

That was until 1961 when the temple land was purchased by a new housing trust designed to tear down old buildings and create level after level of stone and brick apartments that would appeal to new, working-class New Yorkers. Ones who had more interest in TV sets than Torah, and as a result, he no longer had a job. Esther's brother, Louis, had recently moved to the West Coast—first to Seattle and then to Los Angeles, where he settled in the Boyle Heights district. At least once a week, Louis tried to convince Augie to move west through Esther acting as his agent. He had talked about Boyle Heights, the kosher markets, and the fact that the main thoroughfare had been named Brooklyn Avenue as an homage to the Jewish demographic who now were a majority of the neighborhood's populace. It had little effect. Augie liked New York. It was the first place he had settled after the Holocaust, and he saw no reason to move. At least then.

On a fall day later that same year, Esther's doctor only told her that the headaches would improve with medication and rest. Three weeks later, she was in a coma. And by the end of the year, with the sale of the temple nearly complete, Augie nearly jobless, and his wife—who was by all accounts his only connection to the outside world—near the end, the promise of a new start and palm trees began to resonate sweetly between afternoon naps and the constant honks of taxicabs up and down Bayside Avenue.

When Augie stepped off the train and onto the raised concrete platform of LA's Union Station in 1962, the difference in the air was noticeable and welcome. For the second time in his life, he was on the move. Not just the crispness—that part was obvious—but the sense of new purpose and recalibration that it brought.

Louis picked him up in his silver Buick, a bit of "showing off" from a man who could barely afford the rent, but it was a welcome sight to Augie nonetheless. Louis was his brother-in-law, for whom he had always had a sincere fondness.

Three weeks later, after several late-night conversations about the state of affairs, Judaism, and the Dodgers (who, as if they were hot on Augie's tracks, were in the final stages of a move to Chavez Ravine just down the road), Augie set foot in the Breed Street Shul for the first time. Situated just south of Brooklyn Avenue and within squinting vision of the burgeoning downtown skyline, the Shul was absolutely magnificent.

As if by a stroke of fate, the Shul had wanted a janitor, and Augie—partly out of necessity and partly out of a longing for structure again—obliged. He was given his uniform—a gray pair of pants three sizes too big and a short-sleeve, button-down shirt with his name on a patch just above his left nipple.

He wore that uniform proudly every day for eighteen years.

And on a fall day in 1980, nearly two decades after his first steps on the raised platform at Union Station, Augie opened the doors with the skeleton key on his ring and stepped into the storage closet for the thousandth time to get rags. Ms. Posalski had spilled her coffee running to answer the phone in the Rabbi's chambers on the second floor. Again. As he reached for the rags and the clear bottle of pink cleaning solution, Augie smiled. And turned on the radio. ⋆

DAY 1 OF THE CONTEST

“Porciuncula”

Chapter 6

Monday, June 29, 1981
San Diego, CA

Michael "the King" Kingman, resident DJ and faceless voice of the AM station that was hovering around fourth or fifth in the ratings this particular week, had teased for nearly two weeks that the station would be holding a summer contest to end all others. Michael didn't really know if there were, in fact, others or what they consisted of. But if there were, this would be significant by comparison. It would involve cash and intrigue; the rest didn't really matter. In the summer of 1981, for most folks living in Southern California and navigating the early days of a new president and a gas shortage to boot, "cash and intrigue" were quite sufficient.

Radio contests were nothing new to the airwaves of Southern California. But with the desperation of hungrier, holdover AM radio stations like the Mighty 690, the stakes were higher to compete for ears among the growing and diverse suburban constituencies of Los Angeles and its many suburbs, most of whom were defecting to the crisper sounds of the FM side of the dial. Many were left to live their power rock dreams, beautifully perpetuated by mega-stations like KRUZ and KLAA. Stations that tapped into the majesty and spectacle of the golden age of rock. But just as the profile of Southern California grew more complex and nuanced, so too did the musical tastes and demands of those tuning into the radio. Some just wanted to hold on. Stations like the Mighty 690 did that for them rather gracefully.

Michael Kingman had come to the Mighty 690, which had just moved its headquarters from San Ysidro, just north of the border with Mexico, to downtown San Diego. With a transmitter large enough to hit even the extreme reaches of the San Fernando Valley nearly two hundred miles to the north, the station management had justified to its corporate ownership the need for more appropriate corporate digs. Though the plush new offices in the Water Tower near the marina were the face of the station, the heart was the transmitter, perched seventy-five miles to the south on a nameless hillside in Baja, near Tijuana. Just yesterday, in fact, Kingman thought before he entered the studio for the start of his 6 a.m. drive-time shift, the tower had been hit with something, and they had to send one of their local maintenance men to drive over and right the ship before the morning broadcast. Thankfully, he did.

Sitting at the console, he did his mouth stretches (as he was taught years ago), and a red light waited in a panel of indistinguishable switches and buttons before him. "Good morning, Southern California" (with the "good" stretched out to be just under the time otherwise considered annoying), "Michael Boss with you." And by "with you," Boss had always meant it intentionally. Though radio as a medium was clearly giving way to television's broad reach and influence in the late 1970s and early 1980s, Boss had always loved radio unconditionally.

Radio was at a bit of a standstill in those days, he reflected. He had been offered jobs on fledgling local television stations to do news or human-interest stories. But he had always felt a great allegiance to the radio's more antiquated and pedestrian vibe. It was the type of allegiance he hoped would one day pay off. And his voice on this particular morning was crackling with anticipation as a result of that long-held hope in the contest he was on the precipice of launching. But for the next five minutes or so, he was almost the only one on earth to know about it. And he had just enough time between the traffic report and his "go live" time to properly reflect. And take stock. The contest had been his idea alone and was born almost two months to the day prior, during an otherwise innocuous (and boring as fuck) staff meeting.

"We need to do something for the summer slump," Steve Lerman, the face of middle management at the station, said through his clip-on tie and waft of smoke from a newly lit Pall Mall. That is how it started. In the conference room of a slumping radio station, the surge of late-morning traffic on the 5 Freeway (northbound) right out of the window contrasted against a brown and hazy San Diego skyline.

Michael continued to reflect. Time had seemed to stand still before the red light came on.

Immediately recalling his childhood in the undeveloped portion of San Bernardino County, the largest county by area in the continental United States, wedged between the eastern parts of Los Angeles and the Nevada border, Kingman had relished the memories of listening to KMEN radio, a local AM outfit. Playing Cowboys and Indians with the neighborhood kids, he and his friends would listen to the radio station for all sorts of purposes. Sports scores, crop prices, and weather. You name it. But as the waft of smoke finally hit his end of the elongated conference table, he particularly recalled a contest that KMEN had put on when he was eleven or so. The station had buried a gold watch somewhere in the fields east of Mr. Dunnigan's horse farm, and its morning jock, Telly "Tally Man" Watkins, gave folks in the area clues—one a day—as to the whereabouts of the said watch. Kingman and his friends would gather at Jimmy's house right after school and scheme and debate the clues until Billy Gomberg, of all people, figured out with a compass that the watch was buried beneath the feed barn outhouse. Smelly but smart, it was the perfect place to bury a watch—and Billy found it, much to the disappointment of his friends, including Kingman.

"I have an idea," said Kingman sheepishly (but loud enough to be heard) as Steve Lerman and the others looked at him. It felt like pandering. The next five minutes were spent retelling old stories about watches and feed barns, and the suits were sold. The contest that Kingman had in mind was a go, and his sense of pride in ownership quickly succumbed to a panic. But he couldn't help but feel a bit of the excitement he had felt at eleven years old, adorned in a chief's headdress and ready to hunt for a watch.

Two months later, he was at the helm of the new, expensive console in San Diego. The one with indistinguishable buttons and switches. There was no one else to fall back on now.

As the traffic segment predictably wound down, his producer (a young kid in his early twenties out of San Diego State who had only taken the job to increase his chances of getting laid and build his résumé—in that order) pointed directly to him.

The red light finally came on.

He pressed his index finger on the overly done red button with the very predictable "TALK" label strewn horizontally across its bulbous surface. He mouthed the word to himself, as practice, that he would have to get perfect the first time. He was giving the first clue, after all, and whoever figured it out would be one step closer to finding the money that the cousin of a program management intern, who also happened to be a former Brinks security guard, was going to bury somewhere in Southern California.

He whispered it to himself before he went live.

"Porciuncula."

He said it three times in even, measured tones and then closed his eyes. He was ready.

"Welcome to the Summer of Fifty Thousand Dollars." ⋆

Chapter 7

June 29, 1981
Orange County, CA
5:42 p.m.

Sally Lang grabbed her beige jacket abruptly and walked through the empty hallway, out of the bank, and into the Orange County late afternoon air. There was always a sense of shameful accomplishment when she took money that didn't belong to her. Relief as well.

She turned slightly over her right shoulder to make sure her manager, Jeff, wasn't following her, as he sometimes did, under the auspices of "employee safety." In reality, he had nursed a longing for her that wasn't entirely appropriate, even by the workplace standards of the early 1980s. She had given him all the signs of undeniable noninterest, and what was at first a challenge to his ego gently gave way to a subtle disdain and anger over her rejection. He had to balance his fragile male ego with his duties as a bank manager. He knew Sally was a single mother, and although he didn't want to resent her if he was being honest with himself, he did.

"Sally," he said, emerging from the front door, which he had hurried to lock and accelerated his efforts once he saw her. "Do you have a minute?" It wasn't really a question as much as a mandate.

She shuddered.

"You going home to Peter?" he said, delaying and hoping that knowing the details of her personal life could be confused with flirtation.

“Yes, and then dinner, and he has Cub Scouts tonight, so I have to hurry.” Trying to deflect.

“Next week, the auditor is coming,” he blurted out, finding no easy transition in the conversation. She froze in her tracks.

“It’s supposed to be a surprise, as you remember from last year, but I am just letting you and Gretchen know so we can look really good. You know what happened last year. We were off by five fucking dollars. FIVE dollars. That’s just unreal, you know?”

“I remember,” said Sally. She really didn’t. She was consumed by the fact that the sole purpose of the audit, performed by a rather squirrel-faced regional manager out of Pomona, was to catch people like Sally who were either negligent in their counting or, worse yet, embezzling. The same auditor had uncovered what was initially a “short count” in the West Covina branch just six months earlier, and two tellers had received notices shortly thereafter. Last they heard, the proceedings had gone fairly well, and the two were looking at only a year and a half each.

“That was unreal,” she replied out of obligation, trying to turn back to the conversation at hand. As she did so, she turned toward her car, a 1977 AMC Hornet that had been sold to her by her former boyfriend, Glenn Turner, who had, up until last month (when they ended their passionate and often violent relationship), worked as an assistant manager at the Walt’s Wharf restaurant at the end of the Seal Beach Pier. It was not a glamorous job, but he was rugged, paid significant attention to Sally, and, at one time early on in their relationship, had given her a music box as a gift—unsolicited. She had spent the remainder of the relationship hoping for another. It never came.

Jeff just stood in place, waiting for Sally to say something else. She didn’t.

As she put the key in the driver-side door and started to turn it, she heard what she wanted from her manager: “Okay, good night then, and see you tomorrow.” Those words comforted her as she could now be left alone to ponder what she should do next.

Consistent with past pattern and practice, and as if choreographed, she sat in the driver’s seat, used her right hand to grab the shoulder belt, turned on the ignition before actually clicking the harness into place, turned on the radio immediately after, and adjusted the mirror, although it did not need it. As the music faded into commercial, she put the Hornet in reverse and headed north on Orangewood toward her home. Peter was excited for Cub Scouts tonight, as they would be getting some sort of badge.

Fathers and mothers (but mostly fathers, which Sally had noticed) would sit in the back of the church social hall, smells of bad coffee wafting through the space, and smile and clap with the others. She hoped she could do it too without letting her impatience show this time. In all honesty, she was nervous and anxious and could not get the picture of the regional manager out of her head.

As she turned right on Candlewood and into the apartment complex, the commercial paused, giving way to what sounded like a fairly formal station announcement. But it was the voice of "the Kingman" that she recognized from the morning show. Hearing his voice in the evening seemed a bit incongruous. As she scrambled to turn the volume up, she heard something about $50,000 in cash being buried. Still stunned from hearing what was clearly a "morning voice" at night, she was able to make out his description of the contest. One clue a day until Friday. Whoever put the clues together and was able to figure out the location of the buried cash was free to go dig it up.

She had never heard anything like this before, but her skepticism was short-lived. Her thoughts drifted more toward possibility.

Then she heard today's clue. "Porciuncula." Immediately relieved that she had not missed it (since she clearly had not heard it at work while listening to the radio), the word began to appear and then amplify in her mind. "Porciuncula."

Sally had very infrequently paid attention to the specifics of the radio. She would hear certain songs and just assumed the music was a constant score that helped create the aurora of the workday. It served as a distraction to her but not more—something that would occupy space in the stagnant air of the bank count rooms and break rooms where she would listen to banal conversations about haircuts and dates with men that seemed just awful. Maybe she liked the music more than she thought. It drowned out the hopelessness of the lives she and her colleagues conveniently ignored on most days. But this was different. Genuine interest and the seedlings of "what if" began to germinate in her thoughts.

She had to regain focus. Tonight was Scout night.

As she made her way home and parked consciously three feet away from the next stall that the older Russian couple occupied with their Dodge Dart, she calculated how many minutes she had to open the door to her nondescript duplex, change, make sure

Peter was in his uniform, and drive the three miles to the Bay Shore Church for Cub Scouts.

She hated the Cub Scouts, but she liked the normalcy that it provided to Peter. It was one of the few things that made her feel like a normal parent and allowed her to forget about the decisions she had made to provide for her son at the direct expense of the Savings and Loan. It was a choice she had made the first time, with great difficulty, and although it had gotten a bit easier over the last six months, it still weighed on her. Enough so that Cub Scout meetings were perhaps becoming a welcome distraction.

"Peter?" She called out as she walked through the front door and tossed her purse on the coffee table that served double duty as a desk for Peter's fifth-grade school project for the moment.

"Please tell me you're in your uniform already. I really don't have time to hunt through the drawers and find it again."

She walked down the narrow hallway to greet Peter face-to-face but was stopped by the wall-length mirror she had inherited from her cousin Stacy, who had lived in Hermosa Beach for about three months before moving back to Iowa and leaving her possessions to Sally. Reflecting back at her from the mirror were more gray and wrinkles than she had expected. Sally knew that she was aging (a part of working in a profession that she hated, coupled with biological reality), but this particular reflection was startling. More gray. More wrinkles.

Before she could pivot, Peter emerged from one of the two bedrooms in the unit to greet her. Built in the 1940s, it was on the verge of being considered really old by most who saw it. Sally and Peter knew that it was a roof over their heads. And a kitchen to themselves. And stability.

Peter, who had just turned ten and had several of his classmates comment on the small size of his home when over for his birthday party, was still dirty from the summer school day, smudge marks on his knees from playing "smear the queer" in the field just to the south of Fremont Elementary School right after the bell rang. It was not a particularly complex game; it was a time filler between the end of the school day and when his mom came home.

"I got it on, Mom," he informed her as she made her way to the other room and began to change.

"Mom—after school, Dalton came over...if that's okay." "That's fine", she replied, since it had already happened, and there was really nothing she could do about it. "We listened to music, and the radio guy (which is how every ten-year-old described voices coming from the radio—either the radio guy or that woman—both about as descriptive as a ten-year-old could get) said something about fifty thousand dollars being buried, and we want to go dig it up."

Sally stopped. This was the second time she had heard about this today, and now it was more than just a passing conversation about the day with her son.

"Yeah, I heard that too, Peter," she replied, partly in disbelief that her son was listening to the same radio station that she was. Placating the curiosity of her son and balancing her need to get clothes on and get to Scouts, she volleyed right back. "Wouldn't that be great?" As if to simultaneously gauge his interest, indulge his preadolescent fantasies about buried pirate treasure, but if she was being honest, also remind him subtly that his father had left them both with nothing and if for no other reason than that it would make $50K—buried or not—seem sweet.

As they arrived at the church, the aroma of two-hour-old (bad) coffee from the industrial burner and the remaining donuts that the first to arrive didn't care for hit Sally as if on cue. She grabbed both, avoided eye contact with Richard Schectler (who was the only other single parent in the group, who, like a cliché she had gone on a date with four months ago, ending in Richard not reading the signals of noninterest), and took the first seat in the last row. Peter and his friends sat in the front of the church hall. The lighting was a bit off that night, and the hum from the dated electrical system forced the den master—Ken Valasquez, a retired PE teacher and weirdly engaging adult with no kids of his own—to speak louder than normal.

"Merit badges are here," he proclaimed. And the kids, including Peter, seemed to perk up.

As Sally began to fade into the distant comfort of the Monday-night routine, she heard the father of one of the boys—Barrett Dickey, whom she had never particularly liked—talking about buried treasure, an odd topic even at the Monday-night Scout meeting.

This was now the third time today she had heard about the radio contest. And Sally didn't take that lightly. As Ken droned on about knots and reprimanded the boys for not properly placing the flags in the church hall, Sally thought about what $50K could do. For her and Peter. And for her dilemma at the bank.

And as Ken Velasquez turned his attention to merit badges, she began to think and plan. And in her mind, she was going over a short list of people she knew who could possibly speak Spanish.

She wouldn't be too direct. At least, that was the plan. She waited until the presentation on merit badges was completed, and the volunteer den mother was talking about an upcoming event.

"Ken. Can I ask you a quick question?" She whispered to him as he sat back down in the audience. "Do you happen to speak Spanish?" ⋆

Chapter 8

June 29, 1981
Orange County, CA

Danny usually pulled into the Santa Ana Speedway parking lot B around 4:45 on race days, but for some reason, he was a bit early today. Ironically, the oval track had been inspired by the one at the Lions Drag Strip, which had been unceremoniously torn up two years before—long after its heyday—and the remnant concrete sold to the nearby Port of Long Beach for use as filler in their new terminal projects. Danny often wondered, as he would pull into the lot on race nights, if the longshoremen who were doing work on the new expanses of concrete, built to accommodate the new foreign ships that were dropping off containers for local consumption, knew the vivid history that lay under the containers of TVs and imported sneakers that were now being laid down and orderly stacked along the piers.

But Danny's attention was drawn to race day. And the fact that there was $25 per win on the line for each race. He would be that much closer, he imagined, to getting out of the racing gig altogether and opening his own mechanic shop in San Clemente. San Clemente was far enough south that he would feel like he had "made it" but close enough to remain squarely in the vibe and glow of the Southern California beach scene that he had come to love.

The Ogden family had owned and operated the Santa Ana Speedway for about a decade. They had some marginal success with Speedway (a sport that originated in England and was imported to the blue-collar masses of the US) on rudimentary, makeshift tracks in the high desert of California. In places like Yucaipa and Hesperia, farmhands and burnouts would go and watch brave young souls accelerate into the turns of the quarter-mile oval with no brakes. It was befitting the era, with surfing seeing a similar popularity because of its cultural appeal and cool California roots.

Danny had raced on the track out in Hesperia for ten bucks a race before Mr. Ogden (the son) approached him to gauge his interest in the new track they were building near the Orange County Fairgrounds. Given that his dreams of traveling through Europe or working high-paying construction jobs were all but dashed, the racing life was alluring, if nothing else.

"Yeah, I would be interested," Danny remembered telling the scion of the Ogden family, mostly out of hope for a better commute from his apartment in the OC.

A year later, he started racing at the Fairgrounds in Santa Ana. But he noticed that he was having problems with the third turn. Crashing more often than not, he would slam his bike and himself—hard—into the dirt-soaked white ring made of blended cedarwood that the Ogdens had dismantled and then reassembled from their amateur track near Joshua Tree.

It hurt less and less over the course of the last two years as the races went on, and what Danny learned—like a rejected middle-schooler on talent night realizing that his falsetto version of an Elvis song wasn't quite there but a fan favorite nevertheless—was that the crowd came to expect him to crash. He came to expect himself to crash. And he had mixed feelings about this complacent surrender. Broken bones were the norm. But Danny had no one to help nurse him. Or nurture him. Since high school, he was practically alone. Scattered family and scattered friends. But thoughts of owning his own business helped mitigate the sting. At least he would have something of a centerpiece in his life. His father had passed three years ago to the month, and all of his close friends had gone to college, moved, or were married. Not as handsome as he had once been in the eyes of the young surfer girls lining the Pacific Coast Highway (in bare feet and long, flowing hair, chasing boys and cheeseburgers at the pop-up stands between Torrance Beach and the Manhattan Pier), his passing similarity to Leif Garrett still got him a long way with women. But between the casual dalliances with girls and hanging with a few burnout friends he grew up with, he wanted something more. And racing, at least for now, was a way to get there.

On this particular race night, Danny didn't quite remember why he had arrived so early. Perhaps it was the excitement and anticipation (which he still felt but wouldn't admit to the other racers), but more likely; it was the curiosity that had come with listening to the radio just an hour before as he was getting out of the shower, and preparing to head out the door while wolfing down the remaining bits of a bean and cheese burrito purchased from Los Hidalgos down the street the night before. Fifty thousand dollars could buy a reprieve. And he wanted that desperately. It was a long time since the patina of race days had started to fade—that he first noticed at Lions Drag Strip years ago when he went to see Evel Knievel.

He had not listened to the Mighty 690 much, as his co-riders, the track mechanics, and the various vendors who colorfully populated the racetrack were more likely to listen to the harder stuff. Still, he also liked the break once in a while. New music, ironically, carried with it a certain nostalgia for Danny. Perhaps he was not as sequential in his thinking as others, but somehow, listening to the music that the AM station played evoked a sense of longing in him that he had not known with other music. Constantly feeling like a man born either a decade too early or too late, the music of the Mighty 690 suited him.

"Danny, you're in stall four tonight," he heard the younger brother of the Ogden patriarchy, a fat kid who didn't know as much about the racing business as his dad, shriek from behind the turnstile, well within earshot.

"Bobby S. and Mike F. are in the stalls next to you, and the program is wrong. It says you're in heat one, but you're actually starting in heat two, with the big boys," he smiled. He liked giving Danny shit. He knew Danny wouldn't push back and that by the time he crashed into the wall on turn three—about an hour from now—he would have forgotten all about this little interlude.

Despite the spartan appearance of the prep area, race day brought an electricity unique to Orange County during the 1980s. It was American kitsch, blue-collar hero worship, and California soul all rolled into one. Danny took his Honda X3 and walked it the hundred yards or so behind the sliding iron gate and behind the grandstands, joining the racers who would test their mettle before a beer-drinking crowd of about two hundred people, all of whom paid a hard-earned $7.50 to watch the show. Danny *walked* his bike (there was a fine for actually riding your bike in the prep area) into his stall and engaged the kickstand. Stalls were just glorified parking spots for the riders' bikes. Places for them to tune up, each stall had plastic tarps for flooring, beach chairs for the riders and their mechanics (if they had one) to sit on, and beer cans that served as lines of demarcation from the other riders.

The pit, as it was known, was a festival of caricatures. Worn-out motorcycle fanatics from the Fifties, high school dropouts, gear heads, and parolees made up the roster of about twenty-five of the most blue-collar suburban heroes known. They each had their bikes in separate stalls, along with a menagerie of gear. Like gladiators, they were preparing their weapons, replete with STP oil stains from head to toe. But it was the smell that let the riders (and spectators) know they were at Speedway. Ethanol is a pungent odor and even more so when being flared from the rusted tailpipes of dirt bikes. The ocean sea breeze did little to dilute the strong smell, leaving a distinct odor emanating into the Orange County night.

Before Danny could lay out his suits for the races that night or even take out the two wrenches he would need to tighten the spokes of his aging bike; the pit attendant came running into the prep area. He was holding up a large, handmade cardboard sign with the number 5 drawn in Sharpie. It was five minutes to the first race and time for riders in the second heat, like Danny, to finish getting ready and get on stage.

As he zipped up his leather jumpsuit and sparked the engine to get a good, final listen, he looked to his left and to his right. Mike Fern was a veteran through and through. And Bobby Shane had practically founded the sport, first in England and then here, after transplanting himself and his young bride to live the California lifestyle. Danny liked Bobby because of what he meant and where he came from.

Danny did not like Mike for basically the same reasons. What he meant and where he had come from.

Whereas Bobby had been nurturing to Danny in his earlier years, Mike was obstructionist. And rude. And an asshole on occasion. He was one of those guys who didn't know where the line existed between ribbing and being an asshole—an art that most men figure out by the time they are in their mid-twenties. But Mike didn't.

"I'm missing my fucking wrench for the clutch," Mike shouted out to the entire pit of riders. Some were sitting in chairs, some lying down to catch a bit of a nap with their leather suits down around their waists—all shades of colors and adorned with faded patch logos sewn on by various local businesses.

Mike may have shouted out to the entire pit (and in reality, he actually was missing his wrench), but he was assuming (praying) that Danny had something to do with it, so he had an excuse to continue to be an asshole.

Danny noticed.

"I didn't take it, douchebag!"—loudly enough for his contemporaries to hear—and possibly to laugh.

Mike had a habit of carrying grudges onto the track. And this exchange, short and seemingly innocuous, seemed like a perfect reason to continue that tradition.

Mike Fern walked closer to Danny. And deliberately enough for everyone to take notice.

"I think you *did* take it," Mike replied.

As Danny, conjuring up all kinds of emotions, began to clench his right fist, the pit attendant somehow interceded. He knew that Mike Fern had beef with riders. But the way he looked at Danny was unique. It was as if Mike was channeling all his self-doubt and frustration about being the oldest rider in the group and directing it toward Danny.

"First heat just finished," the attendant said. "Time for you guys to get on the track."

Danny mounted his bike first, slowly releasing the clutch, and rode right by Mike with his left middle finger (the one that was not on the clutch) extended high in the air. Everyone saw.

Mike followed. The other riders (twelve in total for the second heat) were now all making their way toward the track.

Most starting lines in sports are distinct, well-marked, and respected. The starting line at the Santa Ana Speedway was none of these things. It was a series of white cloth flags, cut into jagged triangle shapes and strewn lengthwise along two metal wires stretching from the announcers' table (made of plastic) to the island in the middle of the track. If the anchor poles were not working, which was often the case, the crew mechanics staffing the race would have to fill in.

Danny put on his helmet later than most riders. Something resonated with him in making eye contact—not through a visor—with folks in the crowd. He cherished it.

Danny, who had to remind himself that he drew the third position between Bobby and Mike, began his pre-race routine. Cranking the throttle with his right wrist and checking his helmet visor, he managed to look over at Bobby.

"Don't worry about that guy," Bobby tried to calm Danny down. "He's just pissed."

"About what?" Danny replied. He could see the starter making his way to the top of the bowed ladder from which he would blow the air horn, sending the riders into a frenzy of turns and wipeouts.

"He's old," Bobby smiled. "That's all."

Noticing that the starter was having trouble getting the air horn out of his pocket, Danny realized he had another few seconds before the start. His thoughts were elsewhere.

He lifted his visor quickly and shouted to Bobby.

"Hey man, did you hear about this fifty-thousand-dollar thing?"

Bobby knew Danny was talking to him but didn't respond at first.

"You mean the buried treasure contest?" Bobby then replied, to Danny's pleasure. "Yeah, too bad I'm going to find it, so fuck off, please." Bobby had a way of insulting younger riders and making them feel part of the family at the same time.

Danny had heard about it, too. About four hours earlier. And it had him mesmerized.

What had him mesmerized was the fact that he knew what the word meant. He knew it the second he heard Michael Kingman say it four hours earlier mid-bite in his apartment. And it was a feeling he hadn't had in a long time.

He remembered his father telling him when he was a child, in preparation for an eighth-grade civics test at Fremont Elementary School, that the original name of the City of Los Angeles was actually "El Pueblo de Nuestra Señora la Reina de Los Angeles de Porciuncula." He remembered because he had received two more points on the test than Dennis Elm, who always did better than him.

And his father was proud, and that was rare.

Somewhere between the thought of Dennis Elm and his father, the air horn went off.

Danny's right wrist instinctively twisted backward, sending the bike hurtling down the long straightaway of the oval track before turn one.

He was in the lead. Sounds of dirt fragments hitting the concrete railings and the smell of warm cycle fuel made his eyes widen. Oftentimes, leading the pack into the first turn wasn't always a good thing. Pitching his cycle sideways violently to the left, Danny felt his knee scraping the surface of the track. He didn't see anyone pass him, so as he righted the cycle to center and sped up to take advantage of the second straightaway, he was giddy that he was holding on to first.

By the time he started to shift his weight to the left again, he could feel something was wrong. Before he could blink, the bike started to vibrate. Shaking and unsteady, he felt more dirt than he should have as the vision of other riders passing him was the last thing he saw before he was thrown and skidding, belly first, along the track and directly into the wall.

He quickly picked himself off the ground, and before the track attendant could come and help him, he was already on the island, watching the rest of the racers finish the three laps.

Still not quite understanding what went wrong, he could feel the hot blood trickling down the right side of his face, where the metal interior frame of the helmet came in contact with his skin. As the other riders finished and took their "slow down" lap, he could see Mike Fern (who had come in third behind Bobby Shane and a rookie) staring right at him. He quickly did an inventory of his motorcycle so as not to give Mike the satisfaction of staring back.

The left-handle grip had been torn a bit, and he was missing a lug nut from his rear tire, but his pride and fear of further harassment prevented him from fixing it right then and there.

Instead, he shook off his suit and walked his bike off the island, across the track, and under the bleacher. Although it was only about fifty yards in total, it was a long walk. He didn't know how much longer he could do this. Racing and crashing were not sustainable.

When he returned to the prep area, Mike Fern continued where he had left off before the race.

"Sorry, man. Looks like you had a loose nut on the rear."

And in that moment, Danny knew three things.

First, Mike had intentionally loosened Danny's lug nut, causing him to fall. How and when were irrelevant (it must have been when Danny went to take a piss before putting on his jumpsuit). But somehow, Mike knew it was just enough to hurt him but not enough to kill him. Distinguishing between injury and death was commonplace amongst the racers.

Second, this was the beginning of a longer feud with Mike Fern that wouldn't end anytime soon.

And third, now that he had figured out that the buried treasure was somewhere in Los Angeles (after all, that narrowed down the search a bit), he was excited at where the second clue (to be announced sometime tomorrow during the Kingman morning show) would lead him. ⋆

Chapter 9

June 29, 1981
East Los Angeles, CA

Augie was called into the Rabbi's study and told to wait, something he had only been asked to do on two prior occasions, neither of them particularly good. The first time was shortly after he had been hired and was asked politely not to speak Yiddish in the hallways—a first for sure—as the congregation was trying to distance itself from its East Coast (and European) roots. The second time was when Ms. Bombeck complained that what appeared to be a tobacco stain was showing through on the pulpit carpet. Augie knew that it was the handiwork of last year's b'nai mitzvah class that had snuck into the synagogue after hours when they arrived back from a dance at the congregation up the road. Two boys had decided to smoke in temple, which seemed cool and irreverent, but the incident ended up with one of the boys, Jason Schneidman, pleading with Augie not to tell on him. Augie obliged and swallowed the criticism from the Rabbi on his inattention to detail rather well.

This was the third time.

As the Rabbi walked in, he motioned for Augie to sit down. Such a display of intimacy was rare for him, who usually made congregants, especially students, stand. Augie complied and sat in the tan, oversized chair that had been lowered a bit so that the Rabbi's chair was higher in both appearance and symbolism.

"Augie, the Shul is moving. We have been fighting for years with the landlord to better our terms, but we just can't."

The Rabbi's words and the sound his teeth made when he talked too fast echoed in Augie's ears. The silence that followed resonated.

Augie immediately turned to thoughts of Esther. He had been broke and without stability once before, just after Esther died when the operation had not worked. Feelings of warm guilt and genuine sadness competed for his attention.

"How long?" Augie asked pointedly.

"Three months," the Rabbi reciprocated with equal candor. "We...I mean, I...will help you with another temple. I'm sure they could use someone with experience and who is a survivor."

Augie appreciated the patronizing this time only.

He began to think and map out things in his mind. His mind raced between feelings of desperation—the kind of desperation he had only known once before in his life. But he also felt a freedom of sorts—not the kind that comes with achievement or accomplishment but the kind that comes with the serenity of knowing the events unfolding before you are truly and wholly out of your control. He walked back into the utility closet from which he had emerged prior to his audience with the Rabbi and sat in a meditative state for a bit amid the ammonia and other cleansers.

Before he had left the closet for the Rabbi's chambers, he had left the radio on, something he did quite often. Augie's radio was a staple of the auditory environment in the Shul. There was singing—for sure—and a deep baritone voice from the cantor was part of that environment as well. The occasional laughter and the kibitzing from elderly Russian Jewish women also. Perhaps that is why Augie enjoyed leaving the beige radio on—perched on the second shelf of the utility closet—just out of reach of the smaller students—to drown out some of the monotony and the reminders of Esther, who sounded (and looked) a lot like many of the neighborhood women who would come to temple.

The radio had been given to him as a present (although used) from the third-grade teacher. She had noticed, between her rants alternating between Zionism and the traffic patterns that caused her to be late, that Augie seemed lonely. He was. And the radio seemed to provide him a bit of solace during those hours in which the Shul stood empty—and silent.

When it came to the physical attributes of the radio itself, there was not much there. Although by 1981, radios had come quite a way in terms of style and presentation, Augie's looked like a hand-me-down from the prior generation—which it was. Beige and faded, it had manual dial knobs on each side and was about the size of a loaf of bread. It also had a longer-than-necessary antenna that seemed to dwarf the limited power of the sound that acutely emitted from the speakers covered by shorn netting. Adjustments on things like bass or treble were out of the question. This radio was straightforward and utilitarian. Turn it on, turn the dial, and listen.

In terms of programming, Los Angeles in the late 1970s, Augie had learned, was not as diverse as the people he walked amongst along Brooklyn Avenue or Soto Street. People in the neighborhood surrounding the Shul were white and brown and shades in between. They spoke languages that were a beautiful cross-section of all continents—and the flavors were not lost on Augie. He enjoyed the smells of the neighborhood, too. Boyle Heights was among the first that could truly be called mixed. Mixed in sights, mixed in smells, and mixed in cultural tapestries that painted a possibility of community.

But the radio landscape of Los Angeles—and Southern California, for that matter—did not reflect that. It was much more rigid. Pop music and others. The other was a mix of harder music that Augie did not understand or appreciate. The pop was just that—a common denominator of music that transcended the neighborhoods outside of Boyle Heights. The power of pop radio was that it was just as accessible to kids surfing in Huntington Beach—forty-five miles down the 405—as it was to kids playing little league up north in the San Fernando Valley. It was a common platform for a hodgepodge of cultures, neighborhoods, and places that were otherwise not common. It was good.

Despite the occasional talk radio segments featuring local politicians and restaurateurs, Augie preferred pop music for that very reason. He liked that, as an immigrant, his ears could hear and enjoy the same music as the bluebloods who golfed at the country club. He felt like it made HIM one of THEM.

And the Mighty 690, for that reason, is where the dial on the beige radio in the utility closet sat for many years. For as long as Augie could remember.

So on that day in 1981, having been informed that he had approximately ninety days to reshuffle an already fairly shuffled life, Augie heard the word "Porciuncula" and that he—like the men who played golf at the country clubs—could find fifty thousand dollars. Why or what that could do for him was not clear. But in that otherwise thirty seconds of transitory time in the utility closet, sitting in a stupor, Augie felt the flush of purpose come over his body. It was a distraction, but one that came timely.

Augie reverted to the pragmatism that made him such a fucking good janitor. He needed to find someone who spoke Spanish. Perhaps by fate, he opened the door and saw Jason Schneidman.

He saw Jason, now fourteen and working on his confirmation practice, walking through the hallway and figured he owed him. Big time. The tobacco stain had almost cost him his job, and he wanted his record to remain as flawless as possible.

"Jason?" Augie muttered as he walked by.

Jason, who was walking with two girls he was courting simultaneously (as was Alex Fishman, his best friend) through the hallways, was embarrassed. It wasn't cool that the janitor knew who you were, let alone asked you to come over to chat. Jason's friends giggled and left him to return to the classroom. Jason immediately thought he was in trouble again, but he was not. He hoped Augie had not found out that it was he (and Alex Fishman) who had stolen his key ring and thrown it on the roof of the Shul three months earlier.

"Jason, sorry to bother you," Augie got out with less of an accent than normal.

Jason was stunned that Augie had clearly not figured things out about the keys and, above that, seemed to be speaking like a peer to Jason.

"Do you study Spanish in your day school? I only know English and Yiddish," trying to get a laugh out of Jason. Augie had heard something about the contest on the morning radio as he was detailing the kitchen from the study group lunch that had been held the day before. What was then background noise had suddenly been made relevant by the Rabbi's revelation. Augie decided that he had just as much chance as anybody to win a silly radio contest. Age didn't matter, and if (when) he found the money, he would head back to New York and give Esther the proper burial he had wanted to do years ago.

Jason nodded and shrugged the words, "Kind of."

"Does the word "Porciuncula" mean anything to you?"

Jason just stared at him. It did not. But he could find out. "I don't, but I will ask, Augie. Don't worry, man, I will find out." Jason didn't know why Augie had asked or why he was about to help the janitor he had only interacted with to make fun of him or displace his keys. But Augie explained about this contest he had just heard about.

After Jason left, Augie stood in stunned silence, broom handle erect in his hands. Jason was going to help him. The mental machinations he had just gone through in the Rabbi's study that seemed silly ten minutes ago were now a bit more lucid.

He was going to figure out the first clue. ⋆

Chapter 10

Tuesday, June 30, 1981
Orange County, CA
2:45 a.m.

Sally usually awoke at 6:45 on the dot, greeted by the morning with a pulsating alarm clock and, depending on the day, somewhat of a hangover. As a result, she would try to go to bed early most days. One glass of wine after Peter was in bed would usually have been enough, but last night, with talk of the impending audit, two were distinctly in order. Peter would come into her bed, like clockwork, at around 7:00, and they would talk about school, the neighbors, and TV shows. Anything but Peter's father, who was not only considered "off-limits" by Sally in any conversation (with Peter or her peers) but slowly fading from her memory. He'd gone back to Iowa, having left one gas station job for another, eventually climbing the ladder of Midwest uneducated mobility all the way to night attendant at the Comfort Inn off Route 35. Not the Interstate 35, which would be a source of pride, but the local business loop, which was considered the wrong side of the tracks for Ames.

Sally had made it a point to direct Peter's attention forward in life, and talk of his father, in her mind, would bear no fruit.

On this particular night, she lay in bed, tired from standing and still trying to reconcile the image of the woman she saw in the mirror earlier with the wide-eyed Midwestern with olive skin and long hair who got off that bus so many years ago. Wide-eyed, that was, before a life-altering event with a date in the summer of 1969. But Sally tried not to think of that too much.

What she was thinking about at that moment was how impressed she was with herself. Impressed that she had remembered not only that she had embezzled more than $25,000 to date (a figure that had grown exponentially in the intervening months and that became more pronounced as the days towards the auditor's arrival crept nearer) but proud that she had figured out the first clue.

As it turned out, Ken from Cub Scouts did not speak Spanish. However, somewhere on the drive home from Scouts, with Peter nearly asleep, she remembered what "Porciuncula" meant. Shortly after getting her bearings in Southern California, she felt comfortable enough to go out with friends—friends she had just met at the restaurant where she was waitressing. On one of those occasions, she had been quite overserved in a dive bar off Beverly Avenue in the company of a date whose name she could not remember. Chitchat had given way to pleasantries, and pleasantries had led to political talk. He was an activist pushing for a dedicated Chicano Studies program at UCLA, and he was regaling her with stories of Aztlán and the origins of Los Angeles—including its historical name, which she had never forgotten and which sure came in handy all these years later.

A strong penchant for improving UCLA academics aside, she had always remembered his kind face. It was a stark contrast to dates that would come later.

And as Peter crawled into her bed (under the auspices of being "too scared of the dark"), Sally thought for the first time that if she figured out four more clues, there might be a way to cover her tracks at the bank. She knew it was a long shot, but she realized this was a possibility.

"Mom?" Peter asked sheepishly.

Sally turned and acknowledged her son. She looked at her clock and calculated how much sleep she would get before the alarm rang, forcing her to get out of bed, get him dressed, drop him at school, and walk through the bank's doors in Orange County.

What Sally didn't realize, as she finally drifted off to sleep, was that about five and a half hours from now, a young student she had never met would walk into his Spanish class at Rogers Junior High School and ask his teacher, Mrs. Binder, to help him figure out the same clue. And that student would share it with a janitor at a temple in East Los Angeles that she had never heard of. And the three of them, along with a down-and-out motorcycle racer who lived about thirteen miles to her east, would all be anxiously awaiting the next clue. ⋆

DAY 2 OF THE CONTEST

"Xystos"

Chapter II

Tuesday, June 30, 1981
San Diego, CA

Michael Kingman, still feeling sufficiently proud of himself for properly enunciating the word "Porciuncula" only the day before, needed another clue. What he hadn't shared with management, other than where the money should ultimately be buried, was that he didn't have the exact clues on how to get people there. Candidly, he was going to make it up as he went along. And he was fine with that.

Carefully balancing the stresses of having to deliver for his bosses and the need to muster up some seldom-used creativity, he had to come up with something. A means to an end. As long as he pointed people in the right direction with enough difficulty to weed out the majority of listeners, he would avoid what Steve Lerman worried about—a hundred people showing up with pitchforks and torches to dig up money that wasn't there.

But it would be there. And he was going to piece together enough of a puzzle to make it so.

Los Angeles would narrow the area a bit for those who figured out the first clue, but he needed something a bit more specific this time, if for no other reason than to stall. He knew where the money would end up. He just needed to connect the dots for people in a way that would keep them talking. And listening. And in sufficient numbers so that the ratings companies could capture them when they called their homes to do their surveys. After all, that's what this exercise was about. Ratings.

"Mike, did you see the numbers from yesterday?" Ted Lampert, the newly hired and poorly dressed director of marketing for the Mighty 690, asked with just a hint of authority. And an additional hint of optimism.

Ted was Steve Lerman's underling, squarely middle management, and worried about his job. And he also smoked like a chimney.

"Nope," he curtly replied. He wanted to keep up the appearance of being aloof. Michael felt a modicum of satisfaction in Ted's tone. Not wanting to gloat at what was the first sign of a successful launch, he stared straight ahead.

"Well, they're good. Ownership is going to be happy and at least actually come up with the cash."

Michael had been concerned that even though management committed to providing the cash until he actually saw it, there was still a chance of them backing out. After all, he knew enough about the inner workings of the station that commitment with no follow-through was within the realm of possibility. For fuck's sake, he thought, they had a written sign in the station break room that warned employees NOT to dump out the coffee pot until it was empty. "How pedestrian," Michael would often comment to the young female intern.

Michael refocused on the conversation before him.

"They have a question about burying it, though, Mike. Are you sure we can't just put a letter in an envelope or something," he asked between drags of his third cigarette of the hour, which was inevitably staining itself on his faded yellow, short-sleeved Oxford shirt.

Michael Kingman did what he could to not react emotionally. This contest had been his idea and was born out of both nostalgia and necessity. He wanted to respond appropriately.

"Yes, it has to be ACTUAL cash that is ACTUALLY fucking buried. Just like pirate treasure, Ted," he said with a feigned smile and a sarcastic tone that was palpable to everyone.

He relaxed and pivoted toward a bit more of a controlled tenor.

"Hey," relaxing his voice to almost an endearing pitch, "do you remember that scene in *Captain Blood* when Laurence Olivier or whoever the fuck it was found the treasure, and it turned out to be an envelope?"

He grimaced and paused for the reply he knew was coming.

"No," Ted slowly responded.

"Oh. That's right. Because it wasn't an envelope. It was actual fucking treasure."

He turned around quickly, dismissing him, and stared back at the console. In about thirty-three seconds, the red light would come on again, and Mike would have to press it and come up with the clue.

As he pursed his lips, he said it for practice three times, just as before. After yesterday's reference to Los Angeles and today's giveaway, there would only be three more clues. This was a bridge, he thought, to those who were really in the game.

He was a bit worried that this would be the second day in a row with a word from another language. But he didn't really care. It was Southern California, after all, and that would play well.

"Xystos," he whispered to himself.

Although not as difficult as yesterday's word, he almost tripped on the "X" during practice. The red button lit up and he was ready.

Michael Kingman was not a rookie, and he knew how to tease an audience. As the commercial for RC Cola ended and the station played its signature station identification (in both Spanish and English), his mic was live. He had fifteen seconds before Laura Brannigan's "Gloria" would come crashing in with a grand entrance, and his listeners would tune out with agnosticism.

Fifteen seconds was all he needed.

But the audience had changed a bit since the headquarters had moved from San Ysidro to San Diego. Border blaster stations like the Mighty 690, he reflected, were starting to lose ground to more niche stations featuring talk, analysis, and classic rock. Holdouts of pure entertainment were dying on the vine. And he hated it. If this thing was resurrected, he would pin it squarely on the success of the contest. Credit (and a promotion) would be his.

All these thoughts coalesced violently in his head as he said the word again. For real, this time.

The red light was illuminated and cast a colorful shadow on the right side of his face, further textured by the cigarette smoke and tension coming from Ted, who was clearly hovering.

"Xystos."

It was perfect. Slight crackling noises could be heard (some called it static) coming from the airwaves. And he hung on the dead air a bit longer. Part of him could actually feel the word physically transmitting itself through the wire, out on the airwaves and into the ears of Southern Californians. If he tried, he also felt he could hear the palatable sound of the collective synapses of thousands of Angelenos and others pulsating with curiosity. And hope. ⋆

Chapter 12

August 3, 1968
Manhattan Beach, CA

Sally had just arrived in Southern California and didn't know where to begin. She knew moving out West was the best she could have done for herself. The daughter of a department store salesman who drank too much and a substitute schoolteacher who drank even more, she didn't stand a chance really and knew from a young age that Ames, Iowa, was not her "forever home."

By about the fourth grade, it dawned on Sally that her family was a bit different from the others. Where girls in her school class attended organized birthday parties with invitations and favors, her annual celebrations were more of the impromptu type, if and when her parents remembered.

By high school, she was virtually self-sufficient, but not by her own choosing and not in a manner that showcased any sustainable independence. It was done mostly out of necessity. Boys were never really a thing, especially any who garnered interest from Sally. And so it came to be that about forty-five minutes after she left the stage of Sherman Webber High School on the eastern part of Ames, Iowa, in 1967, she was gone for good.

Rusted but still hinged solidly to the frame, the driver-side door of the VW Beetle her grandfather had left her made an echo as she closed it for the last time in her parent's driveway, cap and gown still in the back seat, and headed south on the I-35 to Interstate 80, took a right, and headed continuously West.

Years later, still alone in a new city, she needed a real job. Waitressing part-time at The Kettle in Manhattan Beach, shoveling Bloody Marys to neo-hippies and surfer burnouts, could only get you so far. But she liked that she could see the elongated, wooden Pier from the restaurant patio. It reminded her, especially on later shifts, that she had at least left Ames. The Pier jutted out into the rich blue Pacific like an alluring carnival ride, and she was mesmerized—almost childlike—when she looked at it. The tips at The Kettle were good, but when her coworker, a former transient soul from just outside of Oxford, Mississippi, said the bank was hiring tellers with no experience and a willingness to train, she had to jump.

Three weeks into the training at Great West Bank, she was feeling accomplished. So much so that she returned to The Kettle late on a Thursday evening to catch up and brag a bit with her former coworkers. She could do that now that she was getting a check instead of cash to support herself. The other waitresses at The Kettle listened to her with a bit of jealousy and condescension. That was except for Neil G, whose full last name she never learned. Only that he had started as a host and worked his way up to manager. He had always taken an interest in Sally, and she him. He had sandy blond hair, much like the older guys who would come into The Kettle after a morning surf session, smelling of board wax and salt water. But he would smile at her in a way that made her pause.

When she had reached her quota of self-promotion for the night (and the others at The Kettle had reached theirs), everyone went back to work, leaving Sally and Neil alone for the first time. He asked her out to dinner the following week, and she said yes.

Sally smiled and walked out of the restaurant into the sounds of the cascading surf break and the giddiness that only someone from Ames, Iowa, who took a chance on moving to Southern California in the late 1960s, would understand. ⋆

Chapter 13

Tuesday, June 30, 1981
Orange County, CA
8:10 a.m.

Danny woke up sore—as he did most days. But the added sting of the Mike F. situation and the hopeful prospect of figuring out the rest of the clues in the contest got him out of bed.

Even before his morning piss, he turned on the radio in a mechanical and deliberate fashion. And as if orchestrated by a higher being, he heard Michael Kingman's booming voice, in all its glory, giving the second clue.

"Xystos."

He knew immediately that it was Greek. And when he figured that much out, his mind immediately turned to Elena. Elena was an old girlfriend in the truest sense of the word. Not only had she and Danny dated seven years ago (rendering the relationship by any standard an "old" one). But she was, in fact, seven years his senior (also rendering her "old" given the disparity in their age—even by early 1980s standards).

Danny met Elena while volunteering at a local YMCA pancake breakfast. The kind he really didn't want to go to but the kind that his dad, when he was alive, guilted him into volunteering and helping out with. Danny's dad had been active in many clubs around town. It was what kept him occupied and distracted from the pain of his wife—Danny's mother—running off with a much more successful (at least financially) man. So he volunteered a lot. YMCA, Elks Club—any organization in the area. It was a surrogate for the emotional commitment needed to have another meaningful relationship.

But between serving sausage patties to the older adults and asking if people wanted napkins that morning, Danny noticed a slightly older woman running pancake batter back and forth from the kitchen to the grill. Danny's dad noticed as well.

A few months later, Danny and Elena were an item. They had first gone out, as was usually scripted, to dinners and movies. Dating formality gave way to impromptu walks on the Redondo Beach Pier and other places. It was going well. So much so that on a Saturday night of no particular consequence, Elena asked Danny to a family dinner.

A Greek family dinner, which starkly contrasted with Danny's middle-class white suburban upbringing (divorce and all), was colorful. Between the main course and the dessert, Danny (at Elena's urging) tried to forge a conversation with Elena's grandfather, who asked Danny, in broken English, "what he liked to do." Fearful of breaking from stereotype, Danny told Elena's grandfather (in slow and demonstrative English) that he liked to ride motorcycles (while making a twisting motion with his right wrist) and work out. He didn't really like to work out, but he thought it would impress him in a way that young men try to appeal to the traditionally male side of their romantic interests—and their extended families.

Confused by the term, Elena's grandfather (who understood the motorcycle part given Danny's accompanying gesticulation and mime of his hands on an imaginary motorcycle) motioned for Danny to describe "work out."

Danny reciprocated by mimicking a weightlifter—arms pressing toward the ceiling with invisible weights and overdramatic grunts as if he were playing a slightly modified game of charades.

"Xystos," the grandfather replied. "Xystos." He said it louder, accompanied by a thunderous clap and a laugh.

Danny had never forgotten the word because it was odd sounding—at least to his culturally virgin ears. And the clap resonated with him as well. After Elena explained to him that Xystos meant "gymnasium," they laughed briefly and politely, prolonging what was certainly the most conversational part of the evening. When that had been extended to the point of awkwardness, they then talked about the weather and Ronald

Reagan in broken sentences for the remainder of the evening.

Often having wondered why he chose to remember small interludes from prior relationships, Danny smiled upon remembering this particular exchange, just as the sun reached full morning brightness in his apartment's living room over an early-morning Orange County sky.

But his reminiscences of Greek dinners and word exchanges quickly gave way to the immediacy of his sore back. Not knowing if it was the sun, the pain from last night's crash, or the clue motivating him, he dressed purposefully and went about the chores of the day, trying to piece the two clues that he now knew together.

Los Angeles made sense, he thought, but he didn't know whether Los Angeles gymnasium was exactly what the suits at the Mighty 690 meant. He was also concerned that given Southern California's extensive Greek population, at least some, if not more than a few, would have figured out the first two clues as well.

At about 2:00 p.m., after watching daytime TV through the scattered picture of an old Kenmore black-and-white (still with rabbit ears) and after his second soak in the bathtub, Danny was truly lamenting his inability to put the clues together. But facing the stark reality that he needed to be at the track in about two hours, he began to get ready and prepare his resolve for what had now become somewhat commonplace and routine. He had been doing it (racing and crashing) for so long that there was almost a noble resignation to it.

As a matter of pattern and practice, Danny would head down the flight of stairs and onto his Honda bike. The hours since he had woken into the daybreak of the Orange County landscape seemed like just minutes ago, and the sky was already beginning to thicken and tint. This bothered Danny sometimes—that days seemed like minutes and that they were filled with pain management and desperate hopes.

But the Honda was calling. This was his primary mode of transportation, and he handled it a lot differently than his track bike. That bike was kept at the racetrack under lock and key. On the contrary, his Honda was perched precariously on its left side most evenings after returning from work and deliberately placed halfway into a bed of shrubs surrounding the apartment complex. Danny did this to give the impression that the bike was not worth stealing and for ease.

Danny started the Honda (which would have been considered pedestrian by any track head, and Danny knew it) and hit the 22 Freeway east toward Fairview Drive. He exited, partied in lot B like all the other times, and started to walk in for race day. He was very cognizant of the routine he was a part of. Disappointment would give way to necessity, which, by about this time in the day, would then give way to practicability. He was now racing five nights a week—which was hard on him. But the Ogdens had determined that as long as they could fill 30% of the seats, the races were a go. It was crushing to Danny that his life had become a byproduct of ticket sales. But he needed the money, and he made do.

Like clockwork, he was assigned to stall two again and went through the predictable choreography of unloading his bag, wrenching his bike to race condition, and waiting for a member of the Ogden family to tell him his place for the first heat.

He was about halfway through the prep on his cycle when Mike F. walked in. It had only been twenty-four hours since yesterday's interlude, but it seemed like just minutes ago. While last night's standoff seemed to be driven by male bravado and a bit of history, the tone of tonight's dynamic was pure hate. Mike F. barely looked at Danny as he strode by with his Yamaha C12 on his right. He slowed a bit but barely looked as he went to stall 4. Aware of the goings-on from the previous night, the Ogdens reshuffled the stall order a bit. Bobby S. was in stall 3, providing a welcome barrier between Danny and Mike.

"You are all in race one tonight," said the Ogden boy.

"We are four riders short because San Bernardino is having a sidecar race tonight. That pulled a lot of guys. So we're going to do five heats with all the same guys and rotate positions. Top three times go to the finals, and that's it."

Danny didn't much care for the order of things tonight.

As he zipped up and walked to the oval, he could feel both the tension (from Mike F.) and the lingering effects—both good and bad—of knowing that $50K was possibly that much closer. He still hadn't figured out which gymnasium in Los Angeles they could be talking about. There were hundreds. And no one more notable than the other. But he had until tomorrow to at least try and piece it together. By that time, another clue would be on the air, and possibly more people with better recall and better motivation would figure it out.

Danny took his position and throttled the engine. He knew that Mike F. would be gunning for him. Again.

Danny took the first turn well, as he usually did, then turned his focus to the straightaway and the next turn. The air was a bit humid, the dirt track seemed especially slick tonight, and he knew a crash was inevitable. Danny could just feel it. Either he or someone else, but someone was going to crash. That was what the crowd had come to expect, and so did Danny.

When he first started years ago as an amateur on ready-made tracks in Apple Valley and Victorville, crashes were seen as a sign of fallibility. Ten years of a slow, sobering realization that fallibility was indeed about all he had gave Danny a certain sense of acceptance. He and his fellow racers had been reduced, he often thought, to circus clowns. They were the guys who crashed, and that's why people came to see them.

And to his credit, as if to somehow reconcile his life's shortcomings, he would try and convince himself that at least the crashes were spectacular. Twisted metal and flailing body parts were something to behold, especially against the backdrop of the crisp, clear air of a Santa Ana summer night.

He turned his focus back on the race. As he pitched his motorcycle and extended his left leg to bear the brunt of the second turn, he saw, for a fleeting moment, Mike F. swoop in and cut across his path—quickly and intentionally. Danny didn't have time to react. Before he could even think about straightening out and heading for the third turn, he was down.

For the second time in two nights. And it hurt. Both his lower back and his dissipating sense of pride.

Perhaps as a culmination of the day's events and hard reflection, he decided—then and there, lying on the dirt—that he was through. Not the type of "through" that was immediate, but the type of "through" that was life-altering. This would be the last (or among the last) crashes of his otherwise unimpressive career. He was about the age that others would consider retirement in the traditional sense, but that was not an option.

Before the track crew had time to react and race to help him up, he had time to think. All sorts of thoughts flooded his mind, especially given the adrenaline rush. This was the second night in a row he had hit the ground hard.

But with the pain (and embarrassment) came a clarity. He had it all figured out—in those few moments, lying supine on the oval track. His old neighbor had a repair shop in Torrance that he wanted to sell, and he would fit right in—for better or worse. Working on newer engines for weekend credit-card riders would be a ticket to stability and monotony that he would welcome. It would also not hurt quite as much. At least physically.

As he turned over and rose to his knees, he saw that Mike F. had accelerated at the right time in the final straightaway and crossed the finish line to win the first heat.

It burned a bit, given the fight the night before with Mike. Danny had learned in the last twenty-four hours to reconcile the fact that by removing his lug nut, Mike F. was at least in the realm of hazing. Something that was tacitly accepted by most racers. But the fact that he had crashed tonight because Mike cut him off, both on the track and during a race where they were competing as equals, stung.

And with a bit of hubris, about three minutes after his body was catapulted into the four-foot-high track barrier, squarely in front of the Newport Rib Company banner, Danny was able to get to his feet and was escorted by the track crew (with the newbie pulling his bike) off the oval and under the bleachers, back to the prep area.

The crowd loved it, and the cheers as he exited were a brief salve for the pain he felt in his body. But his mind was elsewhere. On Torrance and repair shops and stability. His friend in Torrance would surely let him buy in. But that would cost money. Ten to twenty thousand, he calculated.

And conveniently, he now knew that $50K (way more than he needed) was somewhere in Los Angeles and somewhere in a gym. Or something of that nature.

"You okay?" asked the young Ogden, who was now back in the stalls to make sure he re-seeded the riders for the remainder of the heats, as Danny was clearly done for the night.

"I'm alright," Danny lied to him.

As he sat in the chair by stall two, his back started to hurt sharply, but it quickly dissipated with a barrage of thoughts and giddiness over what tomorrow's clue would bring. ⋆

Chapter 14

Sometime in the Summer of 1969
Havana, Cuba

Enrique Bohorquez had been scouted since he was nine years old. Still, with over thirty semi-pro and pro scouts from organizations throughout Latin America jockeying for position on the three 11x8 wooden planks that served as the visitors' bleachers during home games (and served as scaffolding for the local Havana construction crews the remainder of the week), tonight was different. Enrique had been born to Venezuelan and Honduran exiles in 1950 on what would eventually become the communist island of Cuba. By the age of fourteen, he had learned two things—that his country, under their new form of leadership, would never be his home and that baseball was what was going to liberate him—spiritually and physically—from the barriers of the island and the social stigma that came with his overly dark skin (as some perceived). Ironically, dreams were what kept him awake at 4 a.m. most mornings, yearning to leave.

His father was never much of an athlete—having competed on the Honduran youth soccer circuit until he was forced to work by his uncles, who raised him in the sugarcane fields. His mother, Pearla, was Venezuelan and never spoke of her home country. Or her family. At least the one she left when she was twelve and boarded a boat with other expatriates to seek life elsewhere.

Havana, for Enrique, was a blank canvas. All he saw was what was not there. What was in front of him—a bearded dictator, a job at a canning factory that allowed his father to work only four days a week for less than a dollar—was not something he wanted to focus on. Not even in his peripheral vision. The dark factory walls and soot-lined nightfalls were all he needed to know that he wanted to leave. But just like that, as a youngster, a schoolmate had inadvertently left his faded brown "Eddie Mayo" glove on the dirt road just south of Enrique's father's property (likely bounced out when the young boy was riding his bike along the rocky path). It was a Wednesday, Enrique remembered. And from that day until this night in 1969—thousands of catches later, hundreds of drills by local youth coaches who introduced him to the game, hours of lectures by his very Catholic father and mother at the dinner table on the virtues of the Church—all led to this night.

By his rough count, partially blurred by the makeshift headlights that were being used to illuminate the field in the southwest part of the city—where the true baseball prodigies played and auditioned before white men with jackets that bore the name of what were to most Cubans just mythical Western icons—Yankees, Indians, White Sox—there were about thirty-two scouts there to see him.

And more specifically, they were clamoring to see him hit.

He had been groomed as a third baseman, but his fielding was average. What people liked—what scouts liked in particular—was his ability to hit the curveball. Which means it didn't matter where he played in the field.

Most Cuban prodigies were home run sluggers. Enrique was a surgeon. He could hit with precision (that his five-foot-nine frame allowed), and he was fast. Once in little league, he had been disqualified from a game for his ability to round the entirety of the diamond on routine infield hits. But he started to age (and grow), and the competition got a bit better, the fields a little less dirty—but his speed improved even more. As did his bat work.

And tonight, he would show the scouts. But there was one he was particularly interested in—Freddy Brigante. At that time, Freddy was a young scout with the Los Angeles Dodgers. His hallmarks were his swaggering bravado, a tan Panama hat, and a half-smoked cigar always on the right side of his mouth, dangling precariously. He had made a name for himself—at least in Latin American baseball—recognizing, grooming, and eventually placing Cuban baseball players in the American Major Leagues. He was a big deal.

And the Dodgers were Enrique's favorite. He had seen Sandy Koufax, Roy Campanella, and others play between the black and white zigzag lines of his father's television set that had to be perched just so on a dining room chair pointing toward the rear of the house in order to catch the broadcast signals from Miami. Fidel Castro loved baseball, but he loved Cuban baseball, and as any self-respecting aficionado knew—even at fourteen—American baseball was a thing all to itself.

Enrique turned his focus back to the humid Havana night and the car lights. He glimpsed strategically enough to see Brigante pull out his notepad just as the player prospects took the field. Enrique, who was in the first tranche of players, cracked a sardonic grimace across his tan Venezuelan-Honduran face, pivoted toward the pitcher, and knew he was in the driver's seat ⋆

Chapter 15

Tuesday, June 30, 1981
Long Beach, CA

Before he died, Jason Schneidman's grandfather made his eight-year-old grandson promise two things. The first was attending Hebrew school at the Breed Street Shul in East Los Angeles (where his father had been bar mitzvahed). Even though it was twenty-four miles from their home and nineteen miles away from the closest synagogue, he (and his mother with a bit tongue) obliged. He often wondered why he spent so much time driving up and down the 710 and 5 freeways when he could just ride his bike to Temple Beth Shalom, which was much closer and where he knew many of the kids. But he had told his granddad he would, so he and his mother were committed.

The second promise was to always follow through on his word. And so, with that second promise in mind, Jason headed to Rogers Middle School, determined to find an answer for Augie. Jason had always been fascinated by Augie in a way that young people are intrigued by the histories and stories that show in the faces of certain adults. Tattoos on forearms also inspire that kind of intrigue, and Jason had noticed Augie's tattoos from the first time he had seen him marching up and down the Shul halls with cleaning products and a sweaty T-shirt two years ago.

Augie asking him about the Spanish word "Porciuncula" was odd, but he felt obligated. So, as he walked to Rogers Middle

School that Tuesday morning, he was determined to see Ms. Leathers before the bell rang. Spanish class served as the perfect opportunity to oblige, and Ms. Leathers (his eighth-grade Spanish teacher with a slightly passable accent and a complexion that didn't lend itself at all to speaking good Spanish) would tell him. He wanted to ask her before classes started as he didn't want people to notice.

"Ms. Leathers?" he asked sheepishly to at least begin the conversation. Their talk then turned to a certain Spanish word and something about a radio contest. Luckily, Ms. Leathers was not only a student of the Spanish language but of Mexican history and culture (she had studied at UCLA and minored in what was called at the time "Ethnic Studies" so as not to be overly offensive to the conservative faculty and admissions folks).

It was part of the original name of Los Angeles, she explained, didactically.

Jason was grateful, thanked Ms. Leathers, and made it to his morning homeroom class, the third desk from the back on the left-hand side, just before the first bell rang. Nobody was the wiser.

As the homeroom teacher faded into the background, talking about the new rules for the school's bike cage, Jason's thoughts drifted. He couldn't wait to tell Augie that he had figured out the first clue, and for some reason, he couldn't wait until Thursday's class. So he needed to call him sooner. He would do it after class if possible, and if not, then later that night. Not wanting to do it in front of his mother, he devised a plan.

The rest of the day was spent going through classes and wondering if he and Augie could really pull this off. His mind wandered to inevitable fantasies about what he would do with that money. He and Augie had not formalized an arrangement, daring not to dream that far. But certainly, Jason opined, Augie was a stand-up guy and would give him at least half. So $25K was what Jason had to work with, at least for now in his mind. As teens often do, especially teen boys, his mind turned to girls. And for Jason, it was one girl: Dana Seaver. She was blonde and beautiful and looked like so many of the surfer girls he would ogle walking down Bayshore Avenue in late-summer afternoons. But she didn't have the bandwidth or desire to notice Jason. She was about as far from the girls at Hebrew school and Shul as you could get. There was always a hint of difference in being Jewish in Long Beach during that time, and at least to Jason, girls like Dana hammered that home.

Sometime during chemistry class, as thoughts of Dana faded to the contest, he became a slightly concerned. Jason's fellow bar mitzvah class members would think it odd, and the Rabbi and other Shul staff would almost certainly raise suspicion among themselves about what their janitor was doing having more than a passing politeness with a student. It's what Rabbis and senior Shul staff did—kibitz. It was a Yiddish term with no direct English translation that either Jason or Augie cared about, as everyone who recognized the term understood it to mean gossip. And they did not want gossip about their newly kindled friendship or the radio contest. Jason thought, at a minimum, it would weed out the competition.

It also made Jason think about why he was going all the way to LA for temple. The process had become fairly routine by this point. Jason's mother, Daisy, would insist on leaving the house by 3:45 p.m. It would allow just enough time to park the car, engine idling, on Roycroft Avenue, giving him just enough time to run across Loma Avenue into the Santiago Drugstore, turn left down the third aisle, and grab a pack of Lemon Heads or Charlie Chans from the shelf, throw the seventy-five cents in three perfectly distributed quarters on the makeshift plywood counter, carefully place the candy between his copy of *Torah Study for the Twentieth Century* and his coffee-stained notepad (his grandfather had visited for dinner one night and spilled coffee on it, and Jason believed it didn't warrant replacing), and be on the 5 Freeway, heading north by 4. Daisy would drop him off on the front steps of the Shul by 4:20 every Monday and Thursday, and he would be in his seat in Ms. Posalski's class at 4:30.

Being late for Hebrew school generally but being late for Ms. Posalski's class specifically, was out of bounds in every sense. But this had become routine, and he was used to it. If pressed, Jason would probably admit that he liked the contrast with his regular school. Seeing ethnic faces and hearing and smelling the culture of his ancestors was a nice departure from the mostly blond and WASP-y makeup of his neighborhood and day school.

The final school bell for the day rang, jolting Jason back to reality, and he packed up his history book and sprinted out of the school and down the front steps. His first stop on the walk home this day, and most days, was Ma and Pa's.

Ma and Pa's had been owned by the Hancock family for over two decades, and they were one of the last stores to provide "credit accounts" for local families—something that Jason took full advantage of on walks home from school. Returning to his home with plastic bags of freshly smoked beef jerky and long, striped, hard candy—Jason's mom bit her tongue and chalked it up to an indulgence that the recent divorce and remarriage of Jason's father would soothe to some extent. The store had been sold by the Hancocks a few years back and purchased by a hardworking Vietnamese family that had only a few years before escaped war to arrive on the shores of sunny California and be housed at Camp Pendleton until they assimilated cautiously into the suburbs of Orange County. House accounts were no longer part of the program, and Jason was fine with that. Occasionally, the family's daughter, a girl with a name he struggled to pronounce and a smile he was smitten with, sometimes worked at the register after school. If the stars lined up just right, it would be on a Tuesday or Thursday during his ten-minute candy run.

This particular Tuesday, it was Cherrie Chans, a name that Jason would recount later in life that seemed oddly racist but tasted like sugar and syrup and cherries—and it kept him engaged during both schools—Hebrew and regular.

As he walked into the house, the radio was playing. His mother was home from work early, lying supine on the beige couch, listening to the Mighty 690. Radio, in those days, was communal and Daisy liked the normalcy and simplicity that it brought.

The timing of Jason's entrance was impeccable. Just as the last commercial faded out, they could both hear a recap of the first and second clues for the contest. Now, Augie's discussion and Ms. Leathers's explanation made sense to Jason. He knew Augie had said something about money, but until that moment, he didn't fully realize that it was about a treasure hunt and putting clues together. About the time his mother noticed that Jason was standing there, listening with her, she rose from the couch, walked around the dining room table (to the left), kissed him on the head, and pondered the beginning of dinner. They heard Michael Boss's clues again. The radio was making a big deal of repeating the clues twice after commercial breaks.

"Porciuncula" and "Xystos."

"Have you heard about this contest, Jason?" his mother asked as if she was in the know.

"Of course, Mom." Then he began to think about why his mother—who by all accounts and to the appraisal of a young teen was, of course, the un-coolest and most pedantic but loving person he knew—knew about not only the contest but the station. The Mighty 690 was replete with Top 40 and, once in a while (which Jason relished), a parody song. His mother would often pass out on the living room sofa listening to a menu of scratchy vinyl on the Panasonic (she really needed to replace that needle, but the Pacific Stereo down the street was charging $15 for the replacement part) of Barry Manilow and Carole King. If Jason heard the *Tapestry* album one more time, he was going to do things he would certainly be charged for. Criminally.

But he overwhelmingly loved his mother, and now, after his dad had left with a woman he remembered seeing at the temple picnic, he mostly felt sorry for her. And protective. And compassionate. He stopped caring why she listened to the station. It gave him something they could talk about other than his dad and school.

His thoughts quickly recalibrated to the contest. And to Augie (and, by default, to Dana).

"Mom, if it's cool after dinner, I'm going across the street to the Koffmans." He didn't share with her (deliberately) that he had figured out the first clue and had a clear plan to talk to Augie about the new clue and figure out what Xystos meant. Moms, perhaps, couldn't be trusted with everything.

"Yeah, that's fine," his mother responded as if resigned.

Truth be told, the Koffmans let him watch *Happy Days* and *Laverne and Shirley* on Tuesday nights, so it was well worth the journey across the street.

After the exchange with his mother, and after homework was done, Jason wolfed down the manicotti-stuffed pasta shells that his mother took so much pride in making (and rightfully so—they were leaps and bounds above the culinary offerings that his friends' mothers would make) and slung the remnants of his history homework into his bag and threw it lengthwise in the entryway to his room. He was out the door into a sky that had just seen the sunset moments ago and turned left.

Long Beach, California, was about as suburban as the term could possibly suggest. It was punctuated with the obligatory fast-food restaurants, old industrial parks, and lots of tract homes. It emitted an ethos that smelled, sounded, and tasted (with varieties of pho shops and taco stands) quintessentially Southern Californian. It also had two temples—Beth David and Star Israel. Both were no more than twenty minutes away, which made it all the more confusing for Jason as to why he had to drive with his mother (or his uncle Mort on an occasional Thursday if his mom was busy) up to Boyle Heights to attend synagogue. He knew no other kids there (most were rich kids from West LA). The fact that his grandfather had attended the temple was of little consolation on afternoons stuck on the 5 or 710 freeways. But he learned to cope.

The night air was inviting and palpably nostalgic, and his three-and-a-half-minute sojourn down the Saltillo tile path, left onto St. Joseph Avenue, and another sharp left up the two concrete stairs and thirteen steps led to the front door of the Koffmans'.

Penny and Larry were like a second family to Jason—and he liked that they were expecting him (this being Tuesday and all). He took his normal seat on the couch in their living room. Waiting about seventeen minutes into the *Happy Days* episode so as to let things settle, he excused himself to go to the restroom. That was the ruse. Making sure that the Koffmans were out of earshot, he called Augie from the Koffmans' first-floor bathroom. The phone cord was just long enough to stretch into there.

Jason dialed the numbers that he had scribbled down—copying them from his mother's red address book under "Temple." Knowing (or predicting) that Augie was likely the only one inside the temple after hours, he dialed the last number.

"It's Augie," the voice whispered. Augie immediately realized that the whispering was probably not necessary. Augie was anticipating the call. The temple didn't normally receive many calls at night—and as Jason had surmised, the only person left in the building at those hours, other than Augie, was the Rabbi, who would normally practice the following week's Torah portion after a few sips of Russian vodka stored neatly and inconspicuously in the bottom drawer of his work desk.

Few knew that Augie lived in the building. He was its sole and seemingly permanent resident.

Augie had once looked for an apartment when he first stepped foot in LA but to no avail. Partially out of charity and partially motivated by the prospect of having someone to keep watch over the building, the Board of the Breed Street Shul agreed to convert an abandoned storage closet to a makeshift bedroom for Augie—replete with a donated Murphy bed and a hot plate. The basement utility closet served as a shower, and after six months or so, Augie felt comfortable calling it (his) home. He would often walk the neighborhood streets at night—

still in his janitor's uniform with his name patch sewn on—and smile at the children. Mostly with distinctive brown skin and increasingly Americanized English, he noticed over the progressive course of his nightly neighborhood walks.

And Augie liked the food—mostly from countries he had never heard of or recognized from his time in New York. Meals would be spent on streetside tables and chairs along busy and noisy intersections of East Los Angeles, contrasted against the towering skyline of the office buildings just over the bridges into downtown Los Angeles. He would often think about Esther. He missed her so.

"Augie, you there?" Jason toned a bit more dramatically as if to wake Augie from sleep.

"Los Angeles," he stated. Emphatically.

Augie paused, not knowing what to make of the non sequitur.

"The word you gave me...it means Los Angeles. And that means we don't have to drive to San Diego or San Bernardino or any of the other Sans, Augie. We are in this thing." Jason paused to let Augie reflect and respond.

Augie nodded his head, although no one was there to see it. And he shook his head with a bit more confidence as he digested the prospect that they had figured out the first clue.

"And Augie?" Jason reengaged.

"The second clue. I heard it today. Xystos. I'm pretty sure it's a Greek word, but I don't take Greek at school, so that one's on you, okay? Can you figure it out?"

Augie paused and didn't want to disappoint his newfound friend.

"I will figure it out, Jason. I promise. See you Thursday for class."

At that moment, they both realized that they had formed—at least cursorily—a bond. And the silence before Jason answered was a testament to that fact.

"Yes. Thursday. That's good," Jason responded before the silence seemed too forced.

"Because I don't think I know anyone who speaks Greek." With that, Jason hung up.

Jason went back upstairs into the dark. The Koffman clan was still huddled around the set (which was still fixed on Channel 7), the room was dark, and he noticed a small Sanyo radio playing in the background. Jason had seen the radio before, but only when he was there in the mornings before school (when he would occasionally drop by to eat a second breakfast), and he could make out the sound between the cigarette smoke and the chaos of the Koffman children getting ready for school.

He thought he heard Penny, who had excused herself from the couch to answer the phone, talking out loud about the radio contest. Jason listened a bit more attentively. He realized he and Augie might not be the only ones paying attention.

Jason thought he heard Penny say "that it was buried under a cemetery in LA," but perhaps he was projecting his excitement onto others. At that moment, Jason felt conflicted between his loyalty to the Koffmans, who had treated him like a son, and his chances of helping Augie.

He also decided that he was going to spend the night at the Koffman house, something that he had done before on occasion and something that his mother didn't mind. It was convenient on some nights, and this was one of those.

The opening credits for *Laverne and Shirley* came on (*Happy Days* had just ended), and Jason eventually drifted quietly to a soft sleep on the green coffee-stained couch with clutched lips so as not to spill his secret into the California summer night. ⋆

Chapter 16

July 1970

Sally hadn't had a date, in earnest, since she moved to California, and to say she was full of teen-like optimism would be an insult to teenagers. She was hopeful. For the first time in many months, her thoughts were not populated with the mundane minutiae of everyday existence—shift hours and gas lines. She felt like she could let go, if for only a moment. Gary would be there in twenty minutes, and what started as a casual perusal of clothing options quickly descended into what was like a courtroom drama from a Tennessee Williams play deciding on an outfit.

Gary knocked on the door, and when Sally answered, it was obvious he was dressed to play the part. Time was a bit fleeting from that point—at least as she recalled it. She would often replay the early stages of this portion of the date in her mind during countless staff meetings at the bank.

The beginning, at least, was always recounted consistently. Gary showing up, the two of them walking in locked gaze down the stairs of her Manhattan Beach apartment that she couldn't believe she paid $250 a month for (a fortune by Iowa standards) and getting into his car.

She had always wanted to go to the restaurants and bars in Santa Monica. Alluring as they seemed during the day, they were downright exotic by night. Everything that she couldn't imagine having—it came as close to the lights that drew her to Southern California in the first place, and the fact that this guy she met was taking her there was affirming.

Gary continued to stay in the character of a true gentleman and opened the passenger-side door for her once they had parked at the cliffside lot just south of Sal's on PCH. It was one of those sites that was a poster-card-perfect depiction of what Southern California felt like. Sea salt aromas and fried clams, surfers running into the shore break hoping to paddle out before the next set came in, and the hum of Corvette engines driving north on PCH before fading into the Malibu landscape. It was perfect, and Sally felt that for the first time since arriving in California, Ames was a million miles away.

They walked into the side entrance and took a seat at a table in the center of the balcony, choreographed perfectly, like a delicate dance over the Southern California shoreline. Gary knew a guy. And he told Sally this. They talked about Ames and baseball and banks and TV shows. Not necessarily in that order, but the attraction between them was real. And immediate.

After dinner, as they left Santa Monica, Gary asked if Sally wanted to come over and watch TV. She didn't, but she didn't want the date to end, so she obliged. She remembered that part of the date clearly and consistently as well.

They headed back to Redondo Beach to a small duplex with a burned orange exterior and birds of paradise around the perimeter.

Gary kissed her almost immediately upon entering his apartment. Sally kissed back. A firm believer in quitting while ahead, Sally began to pull away to enjoy what she hoped would be more conversation or just the romantic inertia of an early infatuation not yet spoiled by the realities of dating and kids and obligations.

But Gary was having none of it.

It was about the moment when she tried to pull Gary's left hand from just below her waistline that she consciously drifted into what her mother had once told her was a "woman's way of forgetting what was about to happen." It is at about this point in the evening that Sally's subsequent recollections of that night stopped being consistent and started becoming a bit more hazy. And sobering. ⋆

Chapter 17

Tuesday, June 30, 1981
Orange County, CA

Tired from Boy Scouts the night before, Sally came home from work and crashed on the couch. The impending audit, coupled with the prospect of being "found out" and potentially losing Peter, was too much for standing tonight. So she needed to lie down.

As she closed her eyes and disappeared into the tactile comfort that the worn couch provided, the barely audible hum of the radio playing from the kitchen made its way into the living room and into her ears. She tried to tune it out, but she perked up (a bit) when she heard the rebroadcast of the morning clue.

And the word "Xystos."

It was a bit of an existential moment for Sally. Odds were that plenty of people, besides her, had figured out the first clue. Figuring out the second would require effort. But then the audit was coming up next week, and she had to get creative if there was any way to avoid being fired (or jail time). Longshots are one thing, but prison stripes and Child Welfare visits are another. She was going to get creative.

Time paused a bit, and all that could be heard in the house was a muffled radio voice, the tick of the wall clock, and the silent sound of anticipation.

"Peter!" She yelled.

"Get your shoes on. We're going for a drive." Still yelling.

On most nights, as she remembered from Peter's early school years, the Santa Ana public library was open until 9 p.m. That meant, if she was thinking clearly, she had about forty-five minutes to park, get Peter inside and adequately entertained, and then find a "Greek to English" dictionary. While standing in the dark looking for her shoes, she realized that the word must be Greek. But if not, at least it would be a good starting point.

As they pulled out of the driveway, Peter in tow and still in his pajamas, Sally felt a purpose and a determination she had rarely experienced. And for a brief moment on that Tuesday night, Sally Lang had convinced herself that there was a way out.

Fifty thousand dollars could back-fill a lot of missing money. ⋆

Chapter 18

Tuesday, June 30, 1981
East Los Angeles, CA
10:34 p.m.

Augie hung up the phone with Jason, feeling alive. With Esther's memory hanging closer to him than usual, he was dead set that they would find the money and that he would return to New York to give his life's love the burial she deserved.

In his head, he was already picking out passages from the Talmud to place on her headstone, which would be in the shade. Perhaps he would find a Jewish cemetery for her proper burial in Brooklyn Heights or a train ride away in Massapequa.

Fluent in Yiddish and passable in German, Augie knew nothing about Greek. He wrote down the word that Jason told him. "Xystos."

He recalled that next door to the market on St. Louis Avenue, where he would buy pickled herring and Lavash bread, was a diner—and the assumption was that the owner, who also doubled as the cook, the busboy, and the manager, was Greek.

Not unlike his other neighborhood walks, Augie donned his patchwork of an overcoat and his Donegal tweed hat and walked east of the Shul toward St. Louis Avenue.

The store/restaurant was still open when he arrived, but there were no patrons. Not one to be shy when money (and the memory of Esther) was involved, he walked into the back, where he found a diminutive Greek man whom Augie assumed to be the owner. They first made eye contact. The owner stopped stirring whatever was cooking in the pot before him. But the Greek's eyes were inevitably drawn, like a divining rod, to the tattooed numbers on Augie's right forearm.

Augie could feel the stare in his bones as he realized he had forgotten to cover them up. Quickly re-engaging the Greek at eye level and assuming he wanted to know what Augie was doing there, Augie started to take off his cap. Before he could finish, the Greek motioned for him to stop. The Greek rolled up the white sleeve of his own shirt to expose a similar tattoo—different numbers but the same ink—on his left forearm.

The two continued to lock in on each other. For the next two or three minutes, no words were exchanged. But then the two talked a dialogue that only two survivors could understand. And for a reason. Pleasantries turned way to translation. And when Augie had what he needed, the Greek invited him to sit.

He eventually returned to the Shul under the glow of a slightly lit sidewalk, and Augie laid his head down on the pillow at around 2:30 a.m.

But he was satiated with both a stomach full of lamb meat and the answer to the second clue. ⋆

DAY 3 OF THE CONTEST

"The First Shot in Defense of Charleston"

Chapter 19

Wednesday, July 1, 1981
San Diego, CA
6:49 a.m.

Radio station management, to a person, was getting impatient. And that wasn't good for Michael. The previous two clues were to be intentionally generic, as they had collectively agreed. Everyone and anyone could now figure out that the money was somewhere in Los Angeles. Rudimentary Spanish and befriending anyone going into or out of one of the many Greek Orthodox Churches scattered throughout Southern California gave you a leg up.

But now, they had determined Ted (perhaps because they didn't know that Michael was the one coming up with the clues) needed to come up with something that would start separating the wheat from the chaff. They had been able to convince ownership that the $50K could come out of their promotional budget for the year. Convincing them to deliver cash to the station by armored car was something that took a bit more time. But they did it. And as Michael Kingman was walking into the office under cover of night to be at his desk by 5:00 a.m., the Bergman armored truck—with two drivers—was parked (engine still running) by the back delivery door. Michael barely noticed, however, as he locked the driver-side door of his AMC Hornet and headed into the building for the morning show.

Michael (and maybe one other employee) knew exactly where they would ultimately bury the money. It was brilliant, he thought. And dramatic. But they couldn't actually do it until the morning of the final clue. Leaving $50K in a semi-public place for that long simply invited too much trouble. This thing would be over in only forty-eight hours anyway, and Michael (who was not a particularly religious man) thanked God for that.

Plus, he thought, if they did bury it earlier than Friday, the station suits, who were already upset about having to go to ownership and pay for that armored car, would have to cough up additional promotional money (that they didn't really have) to pay Sammy the security guy downstairs eight bucks an hour to stand watch.

The whole reason they were doing this sort of stunt, Michael thought as he walked through the lobby—footsteps echoing throughout the empty space—was precisely because they didn't have the type of budget that would allow them to pay Sammy eight bucks an hour. Dreams of working for a larger station in Los Angeles or even in the Bay Area (the competition)—swirled around his head all morning. But he had work to do. He was pregnant on this one and needed to deliver the finish.

As he got off the elevator on the third floor and proceeded to walk down the sterile, hospital-like hallway to the broadcast room, Michael was met by Ted.

"You know they don't want a hundred people showing up and throwing fists to get the cash," he said somewhat didactically.

Michael pondered this statement and was a bit insulted. Did management really think he didn't have the creativity to narrow the field? He may have had his self-doubt, but that was his to own, and hearing it from someone else triggered him somewhat.

He stood in the hallway, one hand on the doorknob to signal to Ted that he was almost trespassing. Hallways and conference rooms were the domain of management. But the broadcast booth was DJs only.

"I'll guess three people tops," Mike said. "Three or four max. After today, the excitement will die down a bit because, as of now, everyone thinks they know where it is. That changes today," Michael said with sort of a subtle, fuck-you in his tone.

Kingman entered the broadcast room, sat in the severely torn, leatherish chair, and stared through the glass. On morning shows like this, there were only three others. A producer (in name only) and two assistant engineers who did the real work. Controlling the mic, bumping music, and ads in and out in perfect sequence. They had all been there at least thirty minutes before Michael. The night shift before them was prerecorded and required only an intern. He usually left at 4:30 a.m. sharp, and the morning crew would arrive. Sometimes with coffee or donuts, rarely both.

Michael stared at them. And they stared back. They were in the dark as much as anyone about what the Kingman was going to say.

Until he said it, and it shot, in real-time, through the airwaves of Southern California. Indiscriminately. Into cars and kitchens and classrooms and break rooms. In poor areas and affluent ones. To ears of all ages and dispositions. Simultaneously. It was a great equalizer of sorts.

"Good morning, Southern California. Waiting for the next clue in the Summer of Fifty Thousand Dollars? Well, here it is."

Pausing only to hear the echoes of his words dissipate in his headphones.

"The First Shot in Defense of Charleston."

He immediately knew (based in part on the quizzical looks from the engineers behind the glass) that it was obscurely historical. And clever.

In Michael's estimation, the two prior clues had really been one-offs—clues that people either got or didn't get—and provided little or no incentive to continue listening. But this one would almost guarantee the advertisers would get the ears they wanted, at least for the next twenty-four hours when they would be back for more. And the station management that Ted was so worried about would see that reflected in next week's numbers. But for this week, at least, they were still skeptical. ⋆

Chapter 20

Wednesday, July 1, 1981
Santa Ana, CA
Early Morning

Danny limped into the foyer of the Cooper Arms building around 7:45 a.m. After the race and the crash, he remembered that the Reno Room Bar was open until 6:00 a.m. and would reopen at 6:30 a.m. Whatever happened during that magical thirty-minute closing used to be a thing of curiosity and wonder for Danny, but no longer. He had sat at the third barstool from the right, nearest the TV and where you could hear the best, from the time he made it there last night to just after 6:00 a.m. When he realized what time it was, he felt a bit guilty. The wonder of that half-hour closing couldn't compare with the stark reality—it didn't really close. And Danny—and two longshoremen who had just finished the hoot owl shift—were there as witnesses.

He stumbled into his apartment, which had stood proudly on the corner of Third and Chapman in Santa Ana for over 125 years and had all but shed its roots as a halfway house for drunks and vagrants during the Depression in the 1930s. Like the building itself, the City of Santa Ana was perpetually on the wrong side of the tracks in a frenetically changing Southern California.

Wednesday mornings at the Cooper Arms building in Santa Ana were sacred for Danny. He didn't have to ride on Wednesday nights, and the peace and quiet of the apartment complex was particularly palpable to him on these mornings, especially nearest dawn. The automated pool filter would usually not kick in until about noon—giving him plenty of time to sleep and recover. Trash days were Thursdays, so even if he forgot to place the trash out in the back alley (which he did most weeks), he still had a day to do it. His refrigerator was usually full enough to ward off any thoughts of going to the grocery store down the street. So, Wednesdays brought with them a sense of calm and restoration that contrasted brightly with the rest of the days in his current life.

But this Wednesday would prove to be a bit different.

He wanted to wake up early—even though he didn't have to. Having figured out two clues in a five-clue puzzle that could lead him to much-needed cash (and a route to escape the pains of the track life) made sleeping in a bit less attractive.

And so around 9:30 a.m. (knowing that Kingman would repeat that morning's clue), with the hangover wearing off a bit, Danny put on a T-shirt, shuffled to the Formica kitchen countertop, and sat. He turned on the radio and listened. And he was disappointed. He had no idea what this morning's clue meant. At least not right now. It rattled his synapses a bit, but not enough. Perhaps it was too early.

Whereas Monday's and Tuesday's clues had brought with them a certain confidence in the future, today's clue was a harsh and immediate dose of recognition that the track might be his home for longer than he had anticipated. But he had the rest of the day to figure it out.

As his mind went back to the practicalities of planning a future without $50K (and the fact that his refrigerator wasn't as full as he had hoped and perhaps did require a trip to the Alpha Beta on Seventh and Redondo), he heard a knock.

Knocks on apartment doors at that time of day were rarely good news. Off the beaten path a bit, the Cooper Arms didn't usually attract door-to-door salespeople or political pollsters. Rather, Danny had learned that knocks on apartment doors in the late mornings in Santa Ana usually meant eviction notices or process servers. Neither of which, Danny had reason to believe, were there for him. So, as he rushed to his bedroom to put on his two-tone Ocean Pacific shorts (the cleanest he had available), he shouted.

"One minute, be right there!"

As he squinted briefly to avoid the bright sunlight that was now peering into and between the shades of his $75-a-month rental, he twisted the doorknob and swung it open hurriedly. Whoever this was, he wanted to get it over with so he could return to his day of rest. And TV and beer, perhaps. It was Wednesday, after all.

It was Mike F.

Danny didn't know what to do. His first thought, ironically, was questioning how the fuck Mike knew where he lived. Drawn to the Copper Arms partly because of its anonymity, Danny quickly remembered that as a neophyte on the circuit, Mike F. had actually given him rides when they had "away races" at places like Colton and Pomona. Danny, out of pure reflex, asked Mike to come in. Mike was the last person he expected and was a bit concerned. And perplexed.

Mike was there to settle a score or to ask for some sort of truce. Either way, Danny didn't really care. As far as he was concerned, the damage had been done, and recompense wasn't on the table. At least today.

Danny hoped it was the latter (truce) but was prepared for the former. The sting of the last two nights was still palpable. Danny, not knowing who would blink first, motioned for Mike to sit on his couch, which he noticed at that moment was more duct tape than fabric. Mike obliged. As he began to sit (Danny was still standing), Danny noticed that Mike seemed older than the persona he had come to know (and greatly disliked) on the oval track. Gray streaks of stringy hair were neatly tucked into a Miller Beer trucker's cap and a scuffed leather (like) jacket composed in an awkward alignment against the back of Danny's couch as he postured his back upright to speak.

"You and I are old," Mike F. pontificated, partly as an actual observation of the apparent and partly to diffuse whatever tension remained between them from the last two nights.

"Yes, we are." Danny took the peace offering against his better judgment but conveniently remembered the prophetic words echoed in most eighth-grade history classes about forgiving but not forgetting. In that acquiescence came a bit of surrender, too. And it felt okay for the moment.

With that feeling still resonating in his body, Danny immediately flashed back to Lions Drag Strip in 1970 when he had gone to see a then not-so-well-known Evel Knievel jump thirteen cars in the crisp Southern California air. It was that night that he knew he wanted to be a daredevil. And a racer. And tonight, eleven years later, it hit him like a ton of bricks that he was neither.

He was a crash dummy, and the fans knew it. The serenity of the moment, sitting there with Mike F., allowed him to recognize that. He was also feeling appreciative.

"I'll make a deal with you," Mike F. said.

"I'll stop fucking with you if you help me with this radio thing."

Shocked by the abruptness of Mike's statement, Danny was also put off that someone else was following the contest. After all, this was Danny's path to salvation, and if others were figuring it out, it wasn't just his anymore. That thought did not sit well with him.

"I know you know about it. And I figured two-heads-are-better-than-one kind of thing. Fifty-fifty." He rushed to the ask. He should have taken his time with a backstory or why he needed the money. Instead, Mike F. was nervous. And too quick. And just like that, as if skipping the lead-in, Mike F. extended his hand to consummate a deal, the terms of which had barely escaped his lips.

Reserved to a fault, Danny played a bit of defense.

"Dude, I hate that fucking radio station. You know that. I turn that shit off every time someone plays it in the pit."

He paused.

"Not for me."

Pivoting to the pragmatic, Danny regrouped.

"But my fucking neighbor won't stop talking about it. He told me that the first clues are easy. It's in Santa Monica somewhere—probably at that park near the pier."

The words drew both surprise and opportunity. Danny had to invoke his best poker face.

"Yeah, I got that too..." said Mike F., not wanting to seem stupid.

"But there are a lot of parks near the pier," Danny interjected to feign a bit more ignorance and draw Mike in a bit more.

"Charleston Street!" Mike said and then paused. "Motherfucker." Mike was happy with the conclusion Danny had led him to. "Fucking Charleston Street right by the pier. Too easy, my man."

Danny wanted to give him assurances, so he chimed in.

"Yeah, my neighbor is such a douche. He thinks Charleston means the restaurant down on Pico." In Danny's defense, there was a Charleston Diner on Pico and Sepulveda.

Now that Mike F. had convinced himself that it was in Santa Monica, he needed to figure out where on Charleston Street the cash was buried. So he asked.

"That's where I need your help," he pled to Danny.

Early signs of an emerging smile began to form on the sides of Danny's face.

"I'll help you," Danny said emphatically.

"We'll wait for tomorrow's clue, and then you and I will cruise up and down Charleston Street, that main part on the beach side of Lincoln until we figure it out. Sound good?"

Danny extended his palm, and the smile he had started earlier was now a fully baked shit-eating grin.

What Mike F. didn't know was that Danny's old man, in addition to being an aficionado of the local drag strip circuit, was a baseball savant. And about twelve minutes before Mike F. had knocked on his door at the Cooper Arms, about twenty minutes after Danny had heard the third clue (a rebroadcast from earlier that morning), his synapses that were only moderately shaken when he first heard the clue, were now clear and sharp. He knew (crystallized sometime during that twenty minutes) that the clue was a reference to Abner Doubleday.

The man who had fired the first shot in the defense of Fort Sumter, South Carolina, thus launching the US into the Civil War. He also knew, as Danny recollected from the many lectures his father had given him, that the same man was the inventor of modern-day baseball.

As he shook Mike F.'s hand, he now knew that the money was at a baseball field somewhere in Los Angeles. But there were thousands. Literally. And with that distraught feeling came another.

Danny knew that he would have to crash again tomorrow night. But there was now, barring someone else knowing random baseball trivia, a good enough possibility that it would be among his last crashes.

Either way, he had a plan for Mike F. ⋆

Chapter 21

July 1969
Havana, Cuba

Brigante usually called Enrique on Monday nights, around what he thought was dinnertime. He knew that Enrique—although nineteen—was still influenced by his parents, and the fact that they were both usually home on Mondays helped. This particular Monday, finally, was the night that his parents would say yes—to his moving to Mexico and then Los Angeles—and the final terms would be agreed upon. At least, that's how Enrique had envisioned it.

He was by all accounts the greatest third-base prospect the Dodgers ever had—and the only one signed to a contract who never played a single game in the organization. Rum and deteriorating streetlights had something to do with that.

"You Enrique Bohorquez?" people would often ask on the streets of Havana and its suburbs if they saw him. Even with a passing glance, they recognized him.

Manuel Hernandez, the flashy first-base prospect also from Havana (about three suburbs over from Enrique), got more attention that year than Enrique. Manuel was faster and hit a bit better. In fact, his tenure with the Expos would be long and storied.

But whereas Manuel Hernandez was well-known and proven, Enrique Bohorquez was legendary. Baseball lends itself to embellishment. And to lionize those who couldn't live up to expectations in any other sport. Perhaps it was Americana. Perhaps pride. But there are no statistical entries in the annals of baseball for being legendary. That is more the purview of literature. And art.

As Enrique put down the phone that Monday night, he spoke with his parents.

"I need to do this," he told them. And the rest, as the legend goes, is history.

They even made a minor league baseball card of his likeness before he signed a contract—mostly for his family. But a few had made their way off the island and into the hands of collectors and baseball disciples.

His parents agreed, and off into the Havana night, Enrique went by bike. He was going to tell Solomon Garcia—the little league coach who had taught him the difference between pull hitting and power swing—the news.

But, as the legend goes, he never made it.

Somewhere near what Cubans at the time would consider a busy intersection on the outskirts of Havana, the greatest prospect who never played for the Dodgers was hit on his left side by a car he never saw. And a car, the judge would determine six weeks later, that never stopped.

The next day, there were only two articles written about him. One in the state-controlled press *El Diario del Cuba* and the other in the *Los Angeles Times*.

Bill Perkins was an up-and-coming sportswriter who had been given the Dodgers beat the year before and wrote glowingly (in the five hundred words he was allowed) about the young Dodger prospect fans would never see play. ⋆

Chapter 22

Wednesday, July 1, 1981
Orange County, CA

If Sally was not out of the door by 7:51 a.m. Peter would be late for school, and there would be trouble at work.

And given the late night they both had at the Santa Ana Library, there was a good chance of it.

Sally was still contemplating her good fortune. A Greek-English dictionary was a rarity in public libraries in Southern California, she had come to find out. More prevalent on the East Coast, the librarian explained to her the night before. "Lucky because usually, the other libraries have only Spanish," the librarian—who seemed a caricature with the horn-rimmed glasses and all—had explained.

By the time Sally had figured out the word meant "gym," driven back home, and put Peter to bed, it was the second late night in a row. She now knew that she was one of maybe a few hundred who would have taken the time to piece together the clues and know that $50,000 in cash was somewhere in a gym in Los Angeles.

And that was fine with her. If figuring out the first clue had excited Sally, figuring out the second had encouraged her.

But there was business to attend to. And Peter.

Peter rarely asked about his father, but when he did, she made it a point to engage, even if she would be late. Carpools were something that Sally was not privy to. Being a single mother branded her with a scarlet letter—whether or not the other moms at Lowell Elementary School would openly admit it. That and the fact that Peter's needs prohibited her from having much of a social life rendered her virtually alone when it came to the kid logistics department. Scouts were something she could muster—mainly because it was after regular school hours—and once in a great while, Sally would allow Peter to ride his yellow Schwinn the six blocks to the school auditorium by himself.

But morning rides to school were her sole domain. So, on this particular morning, she was in the middle of her routine. First, the cereal, then the clothes check, and then the homework. Logic would likely direct her to do those things in reverse order, but habit and all.

Peter would normally sit quietly during this ritual—perhaps asking about what time his mom would be home (he knew). And Peter rarely—neither morning nor night—asked about his father. But today must have been different because after the last of the Sugar Pops hit the faux porcelain bowl, he plainly and directly asked his mom.

"Mom, what's the deal with Dad again?"

It was a softball for Sally to answer, pivot, or redirect any way she wanted. But on this morning, she chose to be blunt. Perhaps it was the auditor who was coming and her elevated anxiety.

"There is no deal, Peter." Your dad was someone I knew a long time ago, and I don't have any plans of knowing again—in any kind of real way."

Peter paused—the aloofness didn't mean much to a ten-year-old. She could tell. "But if you want to call him, I'm sure I can find his number." He knows about you and loves you, but Peter—no Christmas presents should probably tell you something."

She couldn't help herself. The digs felt good once in a while.

Peter seemed satisfied—at least for now. And the routine continued. The awkwardness in the air gave way to practicality as focus shifted to homework and chores.

There was a pause between them.

"Yes, Mom—Peter said preemptively—I did all my homework. And yes, Ms. Bastian said I could turn in my 5.2 math late because I need help."

Sally took this to mean he was on top of it, and, given the constraints on her time (and her sanity), this was just fine with her.

As Sally approached the bank, she immediately noticed something was out of the ordinary. She knew the auditor was coming sometime later in the week but assumed—for some reason—that she would be given a heads-up or at least a chance to prepare. Neither happened. And that became readily apparent as she made her way through the parking lot and saw a white Volkswagen Rabbit parked in the spot she normally took. None of the other employees of the bank would drive such a car. She straightened her jacket, undid her seat belt, and walked at a quick clip toward the bank—like a child who knew she was in trouble and wanted to learn her fate sooner rather than later.

Five minutes later, she, a fellow teller named Peggy, and two other full-time tellers were in the back break room for what was the beginning of a grating and droning lecture from the bank's regional auditor.

She wasn't particularly paying attention, and the radio—the Mighty 690—was playing faintly in the background. The bank usually piped the music in through all the speakers—controlled by a radio in the break room and a rudimentary A/V board that the son of one of the older tellers had installed. It was about as cutting-edge as 1981 got.

She began to focus on the songs to avoid having to pay attention to the auditor. It was something by Air Supply, which gave her a bit of melancholy respite from the auditor, who still wore a vest under his suit jacket—about fifteen years behind trend. About ten minutes in and four songs later, her ears perked up.

"We have reason to believe that the monthly count is way off—and I mean—he caught himself so as not to come across as too emotional for an auditor.

"I mean, like five figures."

Sally knew not only that it was five figures but the exact amount. She had kept a running tally in her head for over fourteen months. She felt like telling him—as if to show him up like an overeager pupil—that it was "$26,450." To be exact. For emphasis.

But propriety and a sense of self-preservation prevented her from doing that.

"I am going to start with the vault in the front and then the reserve vault (where Sally knew the money was missing) when I finish," he droned. At least for a modicum of time, Sally felt that the audit sequence worked in her favor. If she could somehow figure out the remaining clues for this radio contest and get the money, she would be home free—assuming a lot of other variables broke squarely in her favor.

But she was stuck. She had figured out the first two clues with the help of the Scout leader and her late-night visit to what was probably the third or fourth most-visited library in Orange County. But today's clue was an enigma to her (she had heard it while dropping Peter off at school earlier that morning). Until now.

"Wait," the auditor said like a record scratching, as if to bring Sally back to the conversation in the room, but he was addressing all the workers. Inconsistent with his persona in the previous ten minutes, the auditor smiled. It became apparent that he was focusing on the faint din of the radio that, until now, had been just background noise.

"Turn it up," he almost commanded.

Peggy obliged, and as she stood up and turned the dial clockwise to increase the volume, Michael Boss's voice was cued and ready.

He repeated the clue that Sally (and others) had heard earlier.

Something about "The First Shot in Defense of Charleston."

"That's easy," the auditor proclaimed, adjusting the awful vest Sally had mocked to herself just moments prior.

"Abner Doubleday. He was the general who fired the first Union shot in the Civil War. Defending Fort Sumter in South Carolina? Anybody? Nobody?" Nobody answered.

But it was the second part that caught Sally's attention.

"He also was the guy who invented baseball," the auditor said with as much smugness as he could muster.

Seemingly unaware of the context in which the clue was given, the auditor continued to ramble on about audit protocols and lunch breaks. But Sally could barely contain the sense of subtle destiny.

Before he concluded with the audit protocols, he couldn't help himself and said, "If I only knew the other clues, I could quit this job." It was meant to be a joke but came across in an almost defeatist tone. Sally was not about to volunteer that she had figured out two clues on her own and now a third, with his help.

She now knew it was a baseball stadium in Southern California—that narrowed it down significantly—and given the often-idle chatter with her boss and Peter's scoutmaster, she could focus on the remaining two clues.

She went back to fixating on the tackiness of the auditor's vest. And allowed herself to dream a bit of what-ifs. The irony that the man who was singlehandedly going to bury her was also the man who gave her a clue to help cover her tracks was not lost on her. ⋆

Chapter 23

Wednesday, July 1, 1981
Belmont Shore, Long Beach, CA

Howie's Market, which had opened in May 1978, may have been considered the cornerstone of Belmont Shore, but Lynn Perry's Pizza—with its faded green awning, chipped wood railing, and pervasive stench of stale spilled beer—was much higher in the ranking of adolescent interests. The pizza was average, and if you happened to go on a day when John O'Callahan (who had dropped out of sixth grade to pursue cooking full-time) was working, then you were almost guaranteed twice the normal allotment of pepperoni. But it wasn't the pizza that Jason and his cohorts went for. Lynn Perry's held the virtual pole position among the other liquor stores, markets, and restaurants in the area in terms of stand-up video games. Selective and refined in their offerings, Lynn Perry's had a constant rotation of the latest games. It was rumored that in 1977, they were one of only three restaurants in the entire state to have a first edition Asteroids game. Soon displaced by Centipede (with the unique allure of a roller ball instead of a push button), they reached their peak sometime over spring break the year before when Track and Field was delivered and set up in less than a day.

On this particular day, Jason rode his bike to Lynn Perry's after school with exactly twelve quarters in the right pocket of the two-tone Ocean Pacific shorts his mother had purchased the month before in their annual preschool shopping pilgrimage. Clothes were purchased for Jason only twice a year—once in late August during the waning days of the back-to-school sale at the Shore Shop on Seventeenth Street in Seal Beach and again just after Christmas when his mother had ample stock to return to the stores after a barrage of ill-fitting clothes were "gifted" to Jason for the holidays. The quarters rattled melodiously in his front pocket with every pedal of his bike—up St. Joseph, right on Second Street, and right again into the back alley. Nobody would dare ruin their reputation, let alone run the risk of parking their bike in front of Lynn Perry's, where the bike rack was. You usually went around back by the service delivery stairs, and if that was full, then across the street in front of Brandon Collier's house. Today was full.

And Jason would have been there anyway, but his pedal was purposeful on this summer day as he knew three things—Lynn Perry had just received an updated edition Dig-Dug game, and Dana Seaver—his obligatory eighth-grade unrequited crush—was going to be there. He had overheard that on the lunch benches the day before. And it was all he thought about.

The third thing that Jason knew that day was that he and Augie were that much closer to finding a shitload of cash. He would see Augie tomorrow, but today was about Dana.

Protocol was everything; you didn't just walk up and ask where you were in line. You would take your quarter (which logically was indistinguishable from every other quarter, but you knew it was yours) and place it reverently on the right corner of the plexiglass. Jason went in and immediately saw Dana. And then he saw Hank Knapick. His feelings virtually canceled each other out.

Hank had never liked Jason, perhaps because he was Jewish or perhaps because Hank didn't need a reason not to like other kids. He came from a broken home where the primary language spoken was insults—and fists, which translated into his outlook on middle-school life. So before Jason could run, Hank hit him with a right fist to the left ear. And he caught a bit of the eye.

Jason dropped to the floor. He hadn't even had a chance to speak or put quarters on the video game.

With blood still trickling down his face and his pride in need of healing, Dana (who had never really spoken to Jason before) asked him if he was okay. In his own way, Jason was able to reconcile the embarrassment of what had just happened with the giddiness of hearing Dana's voice.

And what started as a casual Wednesday after-school sojourn was no more.

As he lay there on the floor of Lynn Perry's Pizza, all he wanted to do was share his good news with Augie. That morning, Jason had figured out the third clue all by himself. Baseball had been a passion of his grandfather's, and knowing that Abner Doubleday invented baseball was almost like knowing that *Happy Days* started at 8:00 p.m. on Tuesdays. He just knew. And with the Greek that Augie had just learned, fate was on their side.

Whereas Jason once would have thought of hanging out with the Shul janitor socially awkward at best (and nearly fatal in the eyes of his adolescent peers), he felt differently now. It was both intellectually alluring for Jason (who never shared with anyone that he was "too smart," as his uncle Mort had often warned him about and cautioned him against showing off) and welcoming. But since his father left, he felt a strange comfort in talking with Augie, perhaps because they were both used to silence or perhaps because of the utter absence of judgment. Either way, Jason found comfort in these thoughts as he righted himself from the floor and smiled at Dana on the way out. She reciprocated.

Jason got to his bike and began to pedal. His pace home began to quicken as he thought less and less about Hank and more about that sweet smile from Dana.

Thursday could not come soon enough. ⋆

DAY 4 OF THE CONTEST
"The Streets of San Francisco"

Chapter 24

Thursday, July 2, 1981
San Diego, CA

One thing that Michael hated about the station (and he hated a lot of things) was that since the recent ownership change, advertising revenue was clearly more of a priority than the music. There was a day in radio, not that long before Kingman started at the Mighty 690, where music was unapologetically front and center. So much so that DJs were often targets of federal investigators for "pay to play" (literally) rackets and such. But those days were not now. And Michael was reminded of that at most staff meetings. And during the ratings reviews with management. And it stung him a bit.

Now that mega-corporations were in pole position over both the revenue and the listenership, they couldn't care less about the musical format (which Michael knew was the hook for listeners deep down). They were also meandering into something called cross-promotion. This concept, as he understood it, came to roost on this particular Thursday in July 1981 when despite his best efforts, management told him that the next clue in the contest had to be a "push" for one of their largest advertisers, KABC television, a local affiliate of the ABC network known for Friday-night horror movies and pimping cheap airtime to local used car dealerships and, intermittently, church fairs.

Michael was furious but not surprised. Until now, he relished the fact that the contest was truly creative. Something that he (and his childhood memories) had manifested and had curated. However, with this new pressure from the suits, the aurora of the contest had pivoted. Tangibly.

Of some solace was the fact that Michael would only stay at this job for another eleven months. He didn't know it at the moment, but about forty weeks from this particular Thursday, Michael would find himself elsewhere. Professionally. He would look back on this past week as a milestone of sorts. And he would smile.

If asked at this moment, however, he would have told you he was leaving as soon as the treasure was found. But eleven months would suffice, given the circumstances.

Since 1972, the local ABC affiliate in Los Angeles was also known for airing *The Streets of San Francisco* with Karl Malden—a salty actor who appealed to a more senior crowd—on most Tuesday nights after the local news. It was their knee-jerk programming response to a growing trend in crime dramas that tended to boost ratings and provide a safe platform for larger advertisers. And they (the advertisers and the geriatrics) both loved it.

Nine years later, the show (which had stopped running original episodes in 1977) was coming back in a new rerun format, and the company that spent $79,000 on advertising last year with the radio station wanted to promote it. And Ted dutifully heeded the call.

He had told Michael the day before that they needed to plug this ABC account into the clue for Thursday, but Michael blew it off. He didn't take Ted's position as all that serious. Clearly, Michael was wrong, and as a result, he not only had to change the clue he originally wanted to provide but divulge the treasure's final location so that he and Ted could come up with a solution on the fly. And they did.

It bothered Kingman a bit that the fruits of his creative labor had to be shared with a man like Ted, but he quickly turned his attention to matters at hand.

Just as the red light on the control board illuminated itself for the second-to-last time in this contest, Michael was pissed. But staid. And resigned.

As if a puppet talking emotionlessly on command, he pressed the talk button and sputtered the clue, grudgingly this time with a bit of sarcastic inflection (that probably only he noticed). No intro, no teaser, and no warm-up. For their part, the listeners were treated to a bland and sterile voice:

"The Streets of San Francisco." ⋆

Chapter 25

Thursday, July 2, 1981
Orange County, CA

Sally had a particular reason to cry this Thursday. Twenty-five percent of it was out of joy (for figuring out the clues to date and knowing that $50K was somewhere on a baseball field in Los Angeles). But the remaining seventy-five percent was sheer anxiety. And a bit of terror that measured the margin of error.

The auditor had thrown down the gauntlet a bit and not gently at that. What was once great in concept (to recover the money and back-fill the cash to hide her embezzlement) was now something like a desperate and precarious reality. It was her only exit strategy, to which an unknown conclusion was fast approaching.

"Sally?" Peggy said, snapping her out of a daze.

Sally looked at her with a blank expression on her face, not really wanting to engage. She and Peggy had worked together for about fifteen months, and Sally hadn't made any particular effort to get to know her. She was a face in the crowd and not an appealing one. There was no incentive for Sally to find any intrigue or likability. Just a coworker. Plain and simple. If asked, Sally couldn't tell you where Peggy was from or if she had a family to support. Nothing like that. She could, however, tell you about Peggy's work habits, that she liked to come into the bank ten minutes early most days and leave on time, that she mostly kept to herself, and that she ate lunch alone most days.

Peggy and Sally were both standing at their teller windows. The morning rush of customers had been processed, and there was no one to talk with. Sally noticed that Peggy was going to break the long-standing protocol and actually engage her in something remotely interesting.

She was right, but not for the reasons she had hoped.

"Look, hon." (Peggy was a bit older and liked to call the younger women at the bank—and some customers as well if she knew they wouldn't get too upset—"hon.") And as she said it, her fiery red hair and focused blue eyes—like something from a country music ballad—were in full effect.

"I know you've been stealing."

The words hit Sally like a jackhammer. Peggy was neither judgmental in her tone nor threatening in her manner. And Sally picked up on that. But as the words hung in the air, Sally did what most people who get caught do, as if reflexively. She looked around to see if anyone else was within earshot. They were not.

Sally smiled, half embarrassment, half atonement. She looked at Peggy to make sure the next words weren't something along the lines of, "And I've told Management." Luckily, they weren't.

"I haven't told anyone," Peggy signaled as if to alleviate what she expected Sally's initial reaction to be. "But if you need help, woman...." Peggy let that phrase linger because it was just colloquial enough to intimate compassion. Sally felt it.

Peggy's tone softened as she finished her sentence. "I am here for you." Peggy let her eyes burrow into Sally's a bit more and then went back to counting the cash in her drawer (or faking it) as a customer with a long beige trench coach, and the stench of the outside air triggered the bells on the front door. It was a welcome distraction to both.

Sally was relieved. Not just by the bells but by Peggy's help in rationalizing to Sally that at least she, as another woman, understood what Sally might be going through. Both the embezzlement and the need to cover it up. And then Sally also faked like she was counting cash. But she wasn't. She was contemplating. She just needed two more days. That was all. But now, this new twist. She scrambled.

Conveniently, Sally had four sick days left for the year. She had been good about saving them up, hoping that they would accrue year over year and then a sympathetic manager (not Jeff) would let her cash them in. It was a thought not without precedent. Maggie Browning, the teller Sally had replaced when she started, drew the ire of the other tellers when she did something similar. So there was that.

But cashing out the sick days was not at the forefront of Sally's mind. It was getting home. Self-conscious to a fault, Sally had done an admirable job of not letting her coworkers in on her subtle twitches, sweatier-than-average palms on most days, and broken complexion. They were tells. But Sally had never been called out by a coworker like this, even if it came across as compassionate.

Hints and allegations from regional auditors are one thing, but a face-to-face direct confirmation is something entirely different. And Sally knew her limits. Sometimes.

And so, as Peggy's conversation with the beige-coated customer could be heard in the background, and with the pungent scent of bank air in her nostrils, Sally grabbed her sweater and walked to ask Jeff if she could go home for the day. It was an unusual move for her but not too out of the ordinary.

She was going to "tell" him more than ask him, really, but that was all in the tone.

About five minutes after Peggy's "hon" comment, Sally was in the car and on her way home. She thought about lots of places to stop, but given that Peter was in school and given that she needed solitude to sort her thoughts out, she beelined for the house.

At the intersection of Euclid and Orangethorpe, about seven blocks from her front door, Sally stalled, and time stood still.

She was at a light and saw a plexiglass pay phone booth on the corner about twenty feet away. At about the same time as she was processing the sight of the phone booth, the red light in front of her, and the green Dodge Gremlin immediately to her left, she thought of her father back in Iowa.

Memories of her father and his "good advice" were scarce for Sally, but for some reason, she had what some people would call a feeling at that moment.

And as a result, she made an immediate right and parked.

Fumbling for quarters, she remembered the number by heart. Iowa was two hours ahead, and so her father, with not much to do these days except be on standby for some adult parenting, would be available (Sally hoped). He was. And as soon as his voice hit the receiver, the tears started to flow. From Sally, that is.

The ensuing minutes for Sally seemed to be a blur, talking to her father in the plexiglass phone booth on an innocuous corner in Orange County. She was an adult herself, after all, and felt like an infant having to dial in for advice from her aging father. But that was just pride and a bit of ego. Her father actually provided good advice most of the time; it just took Sally a few years of "post-high-school pragmatism" to realize that fully.

On this particular call, her dad mostly listened. He had learned to do that while Sally and her younger siblings were growing up. Barking commands and being philosophical weren't really his parenting style. Listening was. And providing feedback when asked.

After Sally had told him that she "was in a bit of a jam at work," her father asked her if there was anything else on her mind. As a former salesman in Ames, he had learned that what people told you and what they actually meant were often disparate things. So, too, with children, and he knew that when his adult daughter called from a California pay phone booth, it wasn't really about a "jam" at work.

And so he deflected. As a result, Sally took the opportunity to walk back from the line a bit and change the conversation. She wasn't really up to telling her dad that she had stolen money for a host of reasons, not the least of which was that she didn't want to disappoint him.

So Sally turned the conversation conveniently toward the radio contest. It was something that she thought her dad would enjoy talking about. What she didn't realize was that her father being home that day in July would help her more than she could know.

Because in about the fourth minute of the conversation (after the pleasantries had gone stale) and after Sally had shared the clues (including the one about "Streets of San Francisco," which she had heard immediately after leaving the bank early), her father came through.

She didn't know that her father was, among other things, an avid baseball fan. A real student of the game. And he shared with her that besides being his favorite show (he was a geriatric after all), the clue must be a reference to the "Trolley Dodgers"—as San Francisco is known for its trolley system. The "Trolley Dodgers," after all (her father tried not to be too pedantic), was the original name of the Los Angeles Dodgers. When they still played in Brooklyn and were known by that name—at least to the diehard fans.

And as the sun began its long descent into the Pacific Ocean, and just as some of those softened rays hitting the Southern

California horizon were cast on the corner of Orangethorpe and Euclid, Sally knew where the money was.

And she began to calculate, even as her father was still talking about something (Gil Hodges and Sandy Koufax). It was only about forty-five minutes from her house to Chavez Ravine and the parking lot of Dodger Stadium. She knew that if she left her house tomorrow at 6:00 a.m., she would be there in time to hear the final clue broadcast live, which inevitably would be the exact location of the money within the stadium. She wasn't particularly excited. She was more grateful than anything else. And a bit at peace.

And as she hung up the phone with her dad, it dawned on her. Had she not stopped at the phone booth, had she not had $1.25 in quarters in her ashtray, she would likely have given up. ⋆

Chapter 26

Thursday, July 2, 1981
Near Downey, California

As his mother drove northbound on the 5 Freeway towards Boyle Heights, Jason's face was still stinging—as well as his ego. The punch had landed somewhere between his left cheekbone and his eye. An area small enough not to matter normally unless on the receiving end of a closed right fist. But it wasn't so much the punch (and resulting humiliation) that bothered him, he thought, as he stared blankly into partially landscaped medians and freeway underpasses. It was the thoughts of doubt mitigating his otherwise unharnessed enthusiasm for the possibility of what could be. The kind of "what could be" that only a thirteen-year-old knew. When you're thirteen, the realities of $50,000 don't quite sink in. But the possibilities do. And rightfully so. And when you're thirteen, you can do things that the pragmatism of adulthood disallows. Like convincing your mother that you need to spend the night in the temple auditorium as part of your Bar Mitzvah training and that unfortunately (or fortunately for Jason's purposes) tonight (Thursday and a school night no less) was the only day they could accommodate him. And so at around 3:45 p.m. in the waning days of the school year (Jason's school got out much later than most other schools in Southern California as they were experimenting with a "year-round" concept that delighted parents and pissed off kids), Jason told his mom that very thing. Fifty minutes later, they were headed into the LA skyline just ahead of rush hour.

While his mom may have been duped, Jason knew the truth. If he and Augie wanted any chance of finding the money, he had to be in Los Angeles first thing Friday morning when the final clue was announced. The final logistics and details could be planned at the last minute. But being in LA (where he and Augie now knew the money was) and being there tonight was imperative.

And as if on cue, at about the point where they passed the 710 interchange (with only about twenty minutes left in the drive), Jason asked his mom if she could turn on the radio. He turned it to the Mighty 690 naturally, and after the commercial about the jeans sale at Miller's Outpost ended, the second-to-last clue was repeated.

"You know," his mom interrupted the beginning of a Greg Kihn song, your dad loved that show."

She looked over at Jason, who was now focused on her. Not because he was interested in learning anything new about his dad (he wasn't) but because he couldn't figure out the clue. Why were they talking about San Francisco when he and Augie had clearly figured out the money was in LA?

His mother was disappointed, but not so much that Jason didn't want to talk about his dad. Most thirteen-year-olds whose fathers walked out on them probably didn't.

But she tried again.

"You know, the opening scenes were great...with the wharf, and the Presidio...and the trolleys."

Jason heard Presidio. But he was dumbstruck by the trolleys.

When Jason was about nine or ten, he often rode his bike to his grandfather's house after school or during the summer. His grandfather was a Russian immigrant and liked only two things. His wife and the Dodgers. He would regale Jason with Dodger history and stories and legends. In fact, his grandfather had been part of the painting crew that had painted Dodger Stadium in the weeks leading up to its grand opening in 1962. Most of the paint crew, as his grandfather told him, comprised of immigrants. Russian, Polish, German. Mostly European but with a fair representation of recent Latino immigrants. They were all members of the local Painters and Allied Trades Union housed on Soto Street in a seven-story building punctuated by iron lettering on the outside. He would go to the union hall with his grandfather occasionally.

And on one of those trips, his grandfather or one of the other painters, he didn't recall, reminded him that the name of the Dodgers in New York was the Brooklyn "Trolley Dodgers." It had stuck with him for years.

As that memory transited from the banal to most relevant, and as his mother turned on her signal to exit the First Street off-ramp and head east to the Shul, Jason knew the money was buried somewhere in the friendly confines of Dodger Stadium. He knew at that moment, with the staccato echo of the turn signal still humming in the ether of the car, that he was either coming home with $50K (split two ways, of course) or exhausted with a long last week of school ahead of him. ⋆

Chapter 27

July 1970
Redondo Beach, CA

When Gary had done what he did, Sally got up, with all the propriety and etiquette her Midwestern roots could muster under the circumstances. She buttoned her blouse and walked through the dimly lit bedroom, an aroma of cigarette stains and mold wafting from the walls, and bounced her way like a pinball down the hallway and toward the foyer about fifteen feet from the front door.

"Sally?" she heard from the bedroom, but she had neither the disposition nor the strength to turn and confront him.

He was still in the bedroom, hoping that what he had done could be passed off as confusion or consent, but neither was true. As she was presented with the choice to walk out or stay, she was frozen in time. She sat on the cold, tiled floor with music coming from the next apartment and a now passed-out Gary in the bed. She was alone with her thoughts, which cascaded up and down like the shorebreak she had come to know. Gary had raped her, and that was a fact that was pulsating indelibly in her mind.

She felt no pain (at least at the moment), no remorse, and no emotion to speak of. She was numb.

Immediately to her right on the faded tile was a stack of what Gary considered to be his library. Three magazines about hunting and a three-ring binder of baseball cards—like something a twelve-year-old would hide away from the world to be brought out and scoured through in private—to revel in the marvel of youthful dreams and what could be. She found it odd. Not the hunting magazines or the fact that Gary didn't have the executive function enough to buy a table to stack them on. Jumbled like the pieces of an unfinished puzzle, the literature seemed out of place. But in her moment of numbness, with sounds of muted Top 40 songs floating on invisible waves through the doors of a hidden building nearby, her stomach still full from a fish dinner in Santa Monica, and all the signs of a horrible and enduring trauma, she began to read.

First, the hunting magazine with the deer on the cover. Then another. And then the binder of baseball cards. She was pretty sure Gary had absconded with it from a garage sale or unpacked it and forgotten about it from a box of childhood mementos. Sally remembered that her younger brother had kept a similar repository of cards—paper monuments to the ideal of a game she never really played nor understood. She was comforted a bit by the distraction in the moment.

As she flipped through them, she saw men in their twenties with mustached grins. They seemed to realize they were at the peak of their lives—quite the opposite of what Sally was feeling on the cold tile. Still not coherent enough to walk out the front door a mere fifteen feet away, she found some odd comfort in the smiling faces of the pictures. She noticed the diversity. Unlike the segregated city she had come to call home, the pages were filled with black men, brown men—men with Caribbean names, and men who looked corn-fed enough to be from the deepest corners of Nebraska. The uniforms were fantastic. Pinstripes and bold letters emblazoned on clean, pressed shirts and caps—some tilted, some donned with a hint of irreverence. She took it all in. Men with names like Leon, Lemon, Cardenas, and Bohorquez.

The cards read like cryptographs that reminded Sally of the Rosetta Stone she had seen pictures of in her high school history class. She couldn't decipher the numbers or the acronyms. ERA, OBP. But she focused on the beautiful iconography. Always with blue sky in the background, the cards also had circle graphics with positions for the men. Most were pitchers. Some infield. All smiling.

Lost in the night and the dissonance, Sally was on the tile for likely an hour. She began to hear traffic on Hawthorne Boulevard, which must have meant that it was close to 5:00 am. Gary was sleeping. How he could do that, she had no idea.

She didn't want to put the cards down. They provided a fleeting solace and a delay from the lifelong barrage of painful memories that tonight would inevitably provide her. The longer she sat there, looking at the fucking baseball cards, the longer she could hit the pause button. It was likely a Chevy with a faulty muffler that shook her out of her trance. A honking horn followed by loud yelling, Spanish aimed presumably at a coworker to "hurry the fuck up, or we'll be late for work" did the trick.

Sally gently placed the card folder on the top of the hunting magazines, just as she had found them, got herself up, and staggered out of the front door to take the long walk home, head held high. ⋆

Chapter 28

Thursday, July 2, 1981
Santa Ana, CA

Fridays were Danny's day off. And that fact would be particularly useful tomorrow when the final clue was given out. On Thursdays, however, he had to race, but the fact that the track didn't open until 5:30 p.m.—three hours later than normal—seemed like a vacation. He enjoyed the respite from Mike F. And the wall.

And the thought of Mike F. (whom Danny had not spoken with since he left his apartment earlier in the week) wandering around random streets in Santa Monica trying to figure out nonexistent clues was pleasing. But he knew that it would come back to bite him. Just not today. And that was fine with him.

So he lay in bed and listened to the radio. The clues had been pieced together, and he was fairly certain where the money was. But that didn't mean much at the bank. Or to the Speedway folks. Reality set in. He had a job interview to get ready for.

It was the first he had in a while, and he didn't really know what to do. He had been approached at the track a few weeks ago by Randall Margain—the local proprietor of "OC TV and VCR" and also a sponsor (on the third wall) of the Speedway. He talked to Danny about coming aboard and working for him and eventually opening up another storefront that Randall had been eyeing in Mission Viejo. Until this week, the thought of selling TVs (and VCRs) had seemed beneath him, if that was even possible, coming off broken bones and bruised egos night after night at the track. But given the fluidity of the radio contest, the pain from yesterday's fall, and the ongoing beef with Mike F., TV and VCR sales—although a bit fluid—seemed an alluring siren call from the norm that had become his day-to-day life.

About two hours after waking, Danny showed up to the interview. It was the first in practically forever. Not counting the time he was fifteen and interviewed to work at the "Sip and Pump" off Highway 33 near Oceanside in north San Diego County—where, had he gotten the job, he would have been relegated to a life of helping casual tourists fill their tanks on the way home from Palm Springs and occasionally cleaning the deep fryer that served only brown food to those who couldn't wait the extra ten minutes to be in Orange County proper and stop for a meal.

His bones had ached so much that he couldn't sit still in the waiting room.

Selling TVs wasn't a "Great Leap Forward" in the evolution of man, but to Danny, it was a way out.

"Tell you what, Danny. I will let you buy your own franchise and set it up right there on the corner. Hell, I will even give you exclusivity so that you're the only one gonna sell these laser-discs in the whole of Southern California. But I need a small partnership match, if you know what I mean. Franchise fee, for lack of a better word," the manager said. He was a man in his mid-fifties who had clearly had several careers (with limited success) before.

Danny was emboldened and escapist. But he wasn't stupid.

About forty-five minutes into the conversation, they eventually settled on a $10,000 fee that would be paid over time. It was more than he could earn at the track but an amount he could cover in spades if he just strung some clues together and wished hard.

He left with the muted satisfaction of having a backup plan for his life and headed up the 5 to return to the track for the evening's races.

He had already been told that he was in the third heat tonight. So there was no guessing. And although his fall at the second turn had been predetermined earlier in the week, he felt like it wouldn't hurt quite as badly tonight—padded by an extra layer of parachute material that, ironically, Mike F. had lent him—and the cushion that only the hope of a way out can provide.

But as he made his way up the 5 (near the San Onofre exit), Danny felt slightly more encouraged than anticipated. What the folks at the Speedway, including Mike F., did not know was that Danny had grown up a huge baseball fan—his old man to thank—and that he was sitting on the answer to the last clue—one that he had figured out about five minutes after it was given earlier that morning, as he lay in bed, before getting up for his interview, still basking in the thought of Mike F.'s misadventures in what he hoped was the late-morning heat of the Santa Monica sun.

He calculated that Dodger Stadium was only forty minutes from his apartment, and if he timed it right in the morning, he could be there as the last clue was given. It would still give him time to stop at Winchell's Donuts on Harbor Boulevard and be a coffee and a half in by the time he arrived off Sunset.

Later that night, as he slid his bike into the hard boards of the second turn (and as he heard a slight giggle from Mike F., who had figured out earlier that day somehow that Santa Monica was a goose chase and probably the reason for Danny being on his backside at the moment), Danny remembered two things.

He had figured out that the $50,000 was somewhere in Dodger Stadium and that tomorrow morning, just as the final clue would be revealed (and his bruises from the fall he was now experiencing would be puffy and sore), he would be standing in Chavez Ravine with the old wooden-handle shovel he had borrowed, but never returned, from Brandon Collier four years prior. ⋆

Chapter 29

Thursday, July 2
Boyle Heights, Breed Street Shul
8:47 p.m.

By Thursday, Augie and Jason were unlikely friends but friends nonetheless.

Wrapped in the warm glow of the hope that the contest brought them both and an affinity for the synagogue that gave them the proximity needed to forge a liking for and bond with each other, they both knew this was likely the last night of interaction for a while. The final clue would be given out sometime after 6:00 a.m. Jason's mom had bought into his story of a sleepover in the Shul—which had actually been real about a year ago (until the Jason Katz incident). The vague familiarity of this to his mother worked to his advantage.

The reality was that wherever the treasure was buried, they would need a way to get there, and Jason was three years shy of even being a possibility for transportation. The MTA #20A bus would give them a chance—as long as the final clue led them to a place somewhere near downtown. Jason was not quite sure where the treasure was. And the bus was unreliable. And cold. And for a thirteen-year-old boy and a Holocaust survivor, it was not the best option.

As the sun began to tuck itself behind the California skyline, Jason's mom pulled up in front of the Breed Street Shul and let the engine idle. Jason heard the door click as if it was an auditory cue to leave. His mother was never good at goodbyes, even for fake sleepovers at the temple.

"What are you guys even going to do for dinner?" she asked, though she was not particularly concerned about the answer.

"I think we're ordering pizza from Zitto's on Sunset. Near where Uncle Mort used to live."

Augie reminded Jason of his grandfather and his grandfather's brother, Aaron. Augie took every opportunity to somehow interject memories into the conversation about anything related to temple, East Los Angeles, or anything else.

Jason just missed his grandfather.

"Okay," she said with a smile and a quick glance at her watch. It would take her about forty minutes to get back home, and her date would arrive about ten minutes later. Just long enough to blow out her hair, put on makeup, and breathe.

"See you in the morning around ten?" she asked.

Jason had no intention of being there at ten. In his mind, he would be well on his way to $50,000 and, more importantly, hopes that Dana would be even more attracted to him.

"Mom, I told you I'm getting a ride home."

"To Long Beach?" She paused with indignation. "Who is going to drive you that far?"

"The Pallatzes live in Bellflower, which isn't too far away, and they have temple service tomorrow and are going to give me a ride home. It's all worked out."

Music to his mother's ears. Jason's mom seemed pleased (enough) that her son had handled logistics, and she drove away.

Jason walked up the stairs into the temple foyer and turned left toward Augie's room. He knocked on the door, expecting his friend to answer. He did not. Jason wandered down the hallway, past the composite photographs of all the Bar Mitzvah classes that had come before him—dating back to 1947 when the Shul had really established itself as more than a social hall for bridge and gin rummy games and meetings of the LA chapter of the American Communist Party, where women who worked in the garment factories downtown would gather to talk about higher wages and better lives.

The faces of those Jewish kids who had come before him were alarmingly and welcomingly similar. Boys with pressed suits and precocious smiles. Girls with coifed hair and their mothers' best pearls. All smart, all beautiful. All full of life.

Jason stopped for a moment and reflected.

"Jason?" Augie was a bit terse as he entered the hallway from the foyer where he had been cleaning. There was work to do, after all. "Come with me."

Augie led Jason down the hallway and turned abruptly into an alcove that Jason and his classmates had walked by hundreds of times without notice. There was a door that Augie opened after finding the right key on his keychain attached by a retractable wire to his belt loop. The cold air hit them both, and Jason knew this was a part of the synagogue he was not familiar with.

"Come down," Augie smiled.

And for a moment, Jason paused. But just for a moment.

They walked down what seemed like three or four flights of switchback stairs, and Augie pulled on a chain light that illuminated what looked like a garage. Or a basement. But it had a door leading out to what Jason assumed was the alley behind the temple where he and Brad Metzger had gotten into a fight two months ago over words exchanged about Israel. Or rock music. Or something else that really didn't matter at the time.

But, aside from the cold air, Jason noticed the maroon Chevy Nova parked there with clean black tires and a beige interior.

Before the smile that only an adolescent boy can know grew to its full strength, Augie interrupted.

"Mine." Augie grinned the shittiest of shit-eating grins and pointed to his chest simultaneously, as if bragging about some kill in the jungle. And taking ownership.

Jason reciprocated and finished his smile. And nodded his head.

His grandfather had almost the same car, which made the relationship among the three of them—two of them present and one not—all the more complete.

They worked through the night, with a small break for two slices of pepperoni and mushroom pizza from Zitto's, to get the engine running. Augie had bought the car from the temple's previous handyman but never used it. Augie knew that that about all it needed was a spark plug—which he kept in gross just to the left of the exit door. He had never bothered to replace it until now.

And at around 2:35 a.m., just about the time Jason had finished his fourth slice of second-rate pizza and placed the remnants to his right neatly on the paper napkin, Augie was already on the next iteration of how he and Esther met.

For his part, Augie was now comfortable enough with Jason (after all, in a little less than twenty-four hours, they would be splitting a significant sum of money) to share the stories. Some of which he had only shared with family and close friends in New York before he left.

Esther and Augie had met at a social hall event organized by the "Sons and Daughters of Kiev," an entourage of Russian-born but American-naturalized citizens living in New York. Jewish, most of them. They danced and exchanged heartfelt interest. That interest grew over the next decade to full-blown love. Love, as Augie shared with Jason, that didn't stop on the Thursday night that he walked out of her hospital room in New York wondering how to fill out the paperwork. Love that didn't stop when he boarded a train to follow his brother-in-law an entire country away to the city of Los Angeles. And love that didn't stop when he had pieced together the second-to-last clue to the radio contest that morning. After all, Augie was in the older demographic that ABC appealed to by showing *The Streets of San Francisco.* And no self-respecting New Yorker couldn't recite the story of the Brooklyn Dodgers and their original name from rote.

Augie waited until Jason had shared with him the story of Dana. And just as Augie was about to share his plans to use the $50K (or his half, at any rate) to buy a new headstone and visit her grave in the Bayside Queens Cemetery, he let Jason finish his romantic epoch first. He did not want to intrude on the prospect of young love with real-world stories of loss. That would come soon enough.

They went to sleep at about 3:30 in the morning. Augie was going to wait to share the news that they would be heading to Dodger Stadium in the morning. No bus. No waiting for the final clue.

And he wanted to let the thought of him and Jason using the spoils from the treasure hunt to pursue true love, each in his own way, percolate in the early morning air a bit longer. ⋆

DAY 5
LAST DAY OF THE CONTEST
"Enrique's First Home"

Chapter 30

Friday, July 3
Orange County, California
3:00 a.m.

As she drifted off to sleep, as much as she could, given all the excitement (and anxiety), Sally Lang knew two things: First, that she would never be the same. Rape was about the worst act that a human could commit on another human. And she was painfully aware of that. But the second thing she knew, by accident and by focusing on the back of a random baseball card some eleven years ago on a tiled floor in a stranger's apartment, was that the greatest Dodger prospect never known was Enrique Bohorquez. A kid from Cuba who died before he took a major league at-bat and who played third base—not catcher, as so many others believed. Including the three strangers who would be making their way to Dodger Stadium about three hours from now. ⋆

Chapter 31

Friday, July 3, 1981
5:59 a.m.

Michael Kingman had felt his lips quiver only twice before in his life. The first was when he was thirteen and had to give a presentation on the Battle of El Alamein to his tenth-grade world history class. He got a C-. To his teacher's dismay, he had left out the involvement of the American troops—not just the British—in the campaign's success. The second was when he got married. No surprise there.

This was the third time.

When the final clue was given, the fate of his entire radio career would be sealed. And he was fine with that. Plans of moving on were no longer the stuff of daydreams. They were a sure thing.

And so he just gave it. No rehearsal. No practice.

"Enrique's First Home."

Dead silence.

He estimated, at least by what the suits had told him, that over five hundred thousand people in Southern California would hear his words, and a few of them hopefully would head with certainty to where the crew had buried the money the day before. As a lifelong baseball fan, he had come up with the final clue himself—one that would separate the moderate Dodger fans from the one or two who would know where to look.

And like a proud father, Michael hit the break button, sending the station to a commercial. Juice Newton was already queued up on the other side of the break, and Devo not long after that. It would give him a good eight minutes to sit back and let the moment soak in a bit. And it did.

And despite all the shit that management had given him, and despite the pressure from corporate sponsors, the pivot away from good music, and the embrace of profit over taste, exactly eleven months from now, Michael would look back on this particular moment and smile. ⋆

Chapter 32

Friday, July 3
East Los Angeles, CA

Sally woke up early. She had told her neighbor that she had an early meeting and that Peter needed to be at school by 8:00 a.m. With her coffee poured, Pumas tied, and the radio turned up, Sally sat in the Dodger Stadium parking lot and waited. Peter would just be waking up, and her neighbor would come over in thirty minutes to make sure he was getting ready on time.

At just about the time she was questioning whether she had left enough bread to make toast AND sandwiches for lunch, she heard the clue echo through the car—with all four windows rolled up, it seemed to boom. As she heard Michael Boss speak the clue (in what she thought was a rather monotone and lifeless voice), she felt the simultaneous rush of painful memories and muted optimism.

She grabbed the Husky shovel from the back seat (which she had taken from the garage) and stepped out of the car. She quickly glanced around the vastness of the Dodger Stadium parking lot in the early July morning to see if anyone else was there. As she began to walk toward the stadium proper, she noticed an elderly man and a boy, not much older than Peter, and a thin, athletic man in his late twenties or early thirties heading in the same direction.

Her pace quickened. For some reason, as she was now at a near sprint toward the stadium, she could only think of Peter and the practicalities of his morning routine. She was okay leaving Peter for a few hours in the mornings. She didn't know he would be ten minutes late for school because the neighbor would forget where she had placed her car keys. But Peter wouldn't mind. Nor would Sally, after she returned, hopefully with the returned dignity and normalcy and stability that the $50,000 would bring. ⋆

Chapter 33

Friday, July 3, 1981
East Los Angeles, CA
6:30 a.m. (approximately)

Most mornings, , Danny was up by 6:00 a.m. The wounds and a sense of purpose wouldn't let him sleep in any later. So this morning, getting up by 4:30 to beat the traffic and park on side streets near Sunset and Stadium Way (which insiders knew was the shortest walk to the stadium) was not a problem. He had his radio tuned and gas in the tank, ready to go, just in case there was another clue. Or worse yet, if he had got it wrong and the money was buried elsewhere.

He heard "Enrique's First Home" and knew where to go. Like others, Danny had heard the stories of Enrique Bohorquez and, also like others, believed that he was the greatest catcher who had ever been signed—but never played—with the Dodgers.

He silently thanked his dad, engaged the emergency brake on his motorcycle, and sprinted up the slight hill toward the centerfield parking lot. ⋆

Chapter 34

Friday, July 3, 1981
East Los Angeles, CA
6:42 a.m.

Augie had been the first to wake up that morning, almost seven minutes before Jason.

He had never known the exquisite joy of a father watching his baby sleep at night, but turning to his slight right to see Jason, his thirteen-year-old friend, mouth agape and snoring thunderously like a cartoon character, slumped on the office couch that he had refurbished from the secondhand furniture store on St. Louis Avenue, sleeping, was about as close as he would get—or need.

"Jason!" he jolted his young friend awake, "We have fifteen minutes."

Jason was well aware of what was at stake and quickly came to. Quickly. The Nova pulled into the alley behind the temple sixteen minutes later. Augie—who was still basking in the glory that the spark plugs had worked—knew the way.

And as they were stopped at a red light on Sunset near Brixton, they heard the clue. Jason told Augie not to worry. His grandfather had told him all about Bohorquez and how he played catcher. As soon as they got to the stadium, they decided they would run to home plate and start digging. ⋆

Chapter 35

December 1965

Danny Baker's father was excited to be racing at Lions Drag Strip. Danny, as a fourteen-year-old, was just happy to be there and mustered up the appropriate amount of pride that a teen could for his father. This night was not unlike other nights when he would come and watch his dad. Usually in the third race, but sometimes later on the card. Regardless, he loved the sights. And the smells. The acrid odor of ethanol meant that it was the weekend. And that his dad would be in a good mood. At least until they got home, and then his attitude would depend on the amount of money he won from side bets with the other racers on finishing order. But on this night in 1965, Danny Baker's world would change.

As Danny got closer and closer to the gate at Dodger Stadium, running in lockstep with a few other random listeners, he focused on something that happened that night.

His dad crashed.

Danny recalled that in all the time his dad drag-raced, his engine had gone out twice, and his parachute deployed only halfway on another occasion (it got caught on one of the exhaust pipes). But Danny had never experienced something as horrific as his dad steering the car head-on into the barricade. And the moment of not knowing whether he would emerge.

As the onlookers jeered and the limited emergency personnel ran with rescue bags in hand towards his dad's rig, he recalled the moment the door was pried open, and he realized his dad was okay.

He stumbled out to applause. And Danny remembered that more than anything else. His dad shuffled over to him (Danny was now standing alongside the medical folks and other onlookers a few feet away from his father).

His dad smiled at him and grabbed his shoulder. He stared directly into Danny's eyes as he uttered words that Danny would never forget:

"It really hurts, son." ★

Chapter 36

Friday, July 3, 1981
East Los Angeles
7:03 a.m.

As Danny, Augie (with Jason in tow), and Sally looked at each other for the very first time, it dawned on them collectively that only one of them would find the money. They were, after all, in the right place and at the right time. They had made it through the parking lot and were now standing at the entrance to Dodger Stadium. A couple of them noticed onlookers but dismissed them almost immediately. They knew, after all, that the radio station would have to have someone there to verify the winner.

But they were there first, not by fate, but by will and by a little bit of cunning. Disparate paths and disparate people now bound by a weird culmination of circumstances and seemingly unrelated events. But regardless, they were all here now. Strangers to one another but united in purpose—at least for the next few minutes.

Could they really be the only four people in all of Southern California to have figured out the clues?

Danny made a move first. Then, the others followed. As the most physically capable, Danny had a good lead on Sally. Jason and Augie brought up the rear—running (or walking as fast as he could, in Augie's case) through the entrance foyer and into the centerfield gate that led to the field. It had been orchestrated a bit. The radio people and their staff had worked with the

Dodgers for weeks to plan this. They expected a few dedicated listeners to show up this Friday morning. They didn't know that it would be only four.

They were hoping for more, and somewhere, Michael Boss—who was told not to attend—was praying that this contest would be enough to save what little of his reputation was still intact. Just enough to land a job elsewhere.

He had often wondered about moving to a rock station in Los Angeles—he hated the music. He preferred to stay with the pop sounds he had grown accustomed to. But reality was what it was. And KRUZ and KLAA and the like were what the next few years held for people in his field. He hated LA but would move if he had to.

Danny made it to the grass first. Dodger Stadium was a beacon of old-school baseball. During the late 1970s, many ballclubs had moved away from traditional stadiums toward what they thought would be more reflective of a new age, new crowd. But baseball wasn't like that, and some of the owners understood. The Dodgers were among them, and there was a vigilant dedication to tradition. And pastime. You could feel that standing in the stadium. It transcended just the visceral patina of the stands and the diamond. It was palpable. And Danny felt it for a brief moment.

He paused in centerfield and knew where he was headed next. Enrique's home was second base. It was where he had played for the entirety of his storied career as a Dodger. At least, that's the way he remembered it. And that's where the money would be. Before he sprinted to second, he looked behind him. Sally, carrying a shovel over her right shoulder, appeared through the centerfield gate and headed toward the field. Danny pivoted and ran.

When he arrived at second base, he noticed an actual base—which was unusual, seeing as no games were being played. A prop, he felt, for the contest and a monument or marker to the treasure that lay beneath.

Sally paused in centerfield with her eyes set on another part of the field from where Danny had started to dig. Part confidence, part desperation, Sally walked past Danny and headed for third base. Danny smirked to himself. Could she really not know where Enrique had played baseball?

Augie and Jason filed in last. Jason would have been ahead of the pack—if it were just him—but he was caretaking for Augie.

A small part of him had come to terms with the fact that his share of the $50,0000—the part that he would use to buy a new jacket and maybe a couple of albums from McCabe's record shop in Belmont Shore—was not as important as making sure Augie did not fall.

It was a small part of him but an important part nonetheless.

They headed to home plate, and when they arrived, they noticed that Danny's hole at second was already about a foot deep. They decided to start digging about a foot in front of the actual plate—perhaps a foot and a half away. No real reason for it other than a hunch. And hunch, sometimes, was enough.

"Jason!" Augie yelled, "Dig here."

Augie seemed to have the confidence of a much younger man. Perhaps motivated by the morning air or the impending fortune, Augie pointed to a spot like an X on a pirate treasure map. Jason smiled. He liked the sight of Augie so impassioned.

Jason, using the limited framework his thirteen-year-old body provided, started digging. He moved dirt and then glanced at Danny across the field. The two locked eyes at one point as the pace of the digging grew increasingly more fevered. Danny would dig, then look at Jason to gauge his progress. Jason, in turn, would dig, then look at Danny. This tête-à-tête went on for a few minutes longer.

The morning air grew a bit more crisp and a bit more cloudy.

Sally, who had finally made it to third base—ninety feet away from where the others were digging—welled up with tears as she realized she was the only one who knew Enrique's true home.

She remembered, with bitterness and now a sense of ironic purpose, that Enrique played third base, as his statistics showed. That evening of trauma and a lifetime of scarring had led to this.

Coincidental as it was, Sally knew that there was a bit more of the divine involved in leading her to this moment. She forced the shovel off her shoulder like a soldier unfurling his rifle and placed it on the ground to dig. Every shovelful of dirt brought tears and a clenched smile. She could feel the warm saltiness pour over her lips and even saw a few drops hit the ground as if to fertilize the moment that would change her life.

After about seventeen shovelfuls of dirt, discarded to her left side in a neat pile, Sally felt and heard the welcome noise of metal hitting metal. It was loud enough for the others—still digging feverishly at second base and home plate, to pause.

They knew.

And with a shared sense of disappointment, they began to shuffle out. And away. Their pace (and motivation) was slower than what had brought them to the stadium just an hour earlier.

Like always, paperwork was involved—which was done conveniently in the parking lot. Something about a waiver, showing her ID, and Sally was left alone (after two obligatory photos that would be used to promote more contests) with a bag of $50,000 in cash and restored hope.

And just like that, Sally was alone. ⋆

AFTER THE CONTEST

Chapter 37

Monday, July 6, 1981

Monday morning could not have come quickly enough for Sally. If she wanted to put the cash back in the vault, she would have to be there early. This whole thing came down to whether or not Peggy would be there ten minutes early—as she usually was. That was out of Sally's control. It really depended on the 57 bus.

She needed Peggy to let her in, and then she would make her way to the break room, adjacent to the vault. She would key herself in, put the $26,450 she had calculated was to be found "lost" by the auditor, and put it in the top tray on the right—part of the bank's reserves, which were counted weekly. She already had it in an Alpha Beta shopping bag tucked neatly in the left side liner of her blue coat.

Sally waited in the parking lot. She didn't know the exact identity of the Orange County Transit Authority driver who made an integral accomplice that Monday morning, but she thanked him nevertheless. Out loud.

As she saw the bus turn right on Orangethorpe, she knew that Peggy was there ten minutes early, and she let out a sigh of relief.

"Hey, Peggy," Sally said, trying to hide her nervousness.

"Happy Monday," Peggy returned with a clear indifference.

Sally followed Peggy in, not too closely so as not to give

away her anxiousness but close enough to take advantage of the full ten minutes before the supervisor showed up.

“I’m just going to head to the break room for a bit.” Peggy nodded in acknowledgment.

“I had a bit of a weekend.” ⋆

Chapter 38

Tuesday, July 7, 1981
Santa Ana, CA

When Carl Dawson arrived at the fairgrounds to sweep the track, deliver the trash to the bins (it was trash day), and get the mechanics' stables ready by 9:00 a.m., he noticed something. Stalls at the Santa Ana track were disruptively messy. Every racer was allotted a 10x10 stall to house not only their equipment, bikes, and tools but anything else they needed, which often meant stockpiles of beer cans, camping chairs, and portable radios. If there was something off about a particular stall, Carl was the first to know. And on this Monday morning, there was definitely something wrong.

Right next to Mike F.'s stall, the third one from the left, there was just empty space. As if someone had come in the night before and cleared it out. But Carl couldn't understand why Mike, a racer with many years of stellar experience and a loyal fan base, would just disappear.

At about the same time that Carl was hovering over the emptiness he had discovered, a young man of thirty (who had only ever wanted to be a motorcycle daredevil like his hero) was boarding a bus in downtown Los Angeles to head east and spend time with his childhood friend Brandon for a while.

The sign on the bus window said "Kansas City," but as he took his seat in row 5, next to a woman who looked over-traveled and tired, he didn't know if that was where he was headed. But it was for now. ⋆

Chapter 39

Monday, August 3, 1981

Augie believed (correctly) that he could fit all of his worldly possessions into a single beige suitcase that had laid dormant on the upper shelf of his closet for over a decade at the Shul dormitory. He felt conflicted that he was right. But packed he was and ready to head to New York at 7:10 the following morning. His brother-in-law Louis's son, now an investment banker at a firm with mostly WASP-y sounding names and headquartered in Manhattan, had been put on the building's maintenance committee just two months prior. Among his first orders of business was to find a new janitor.

The call from the son came serendipitously, a week after Louis had reconnected with Augie for the first time in a long time. They determined that going home to New York was not only the right thing to do but what Esther would have wanted. In the week between the time the Manhattan Colonial Life Building Maintenance Committee decided to hire Augie Kloptman as the new full-time janitor (with no medical insurance) and the time the beige suitcase was shut for the last time in the confines of the Breed Street Shul, Augie had talked to the Rabbi about a severance and said his goodbyes to everyone.

Except to Jason.

Their last exchange came two days after they had left Dodger Stadium empty-handed. It was a typical Tuesday Hebrew school class, and Jason walked by Augie in the hallway. They nodded to each other—Jason to Augie as a sign of respect and gratitude for what had occurred and Augie as a way to say goodbye—in his own way, without hurting the young man he had come to befriend. Jason didn't know it was the last time they would see each other. If he had known, he likely would have gotten over his teen bravado and embarrassment in front of his friends to say a proper goodbye.

Augie smiled and watched Jason turn right down the elongated corridor leading from the classrooms to the sanctuary and thought how lucky he was that he had made a friend. ⋆

Chapter 40

Tuesday, July 7, 1981
Orange County, CA

As the auditor closed his spiral-bound notebook and mumbled something to Brad about no significant findings, Sally was conducting her last transaction of the day.

"Looks like it was just the five bucks...and that could have happened to anyone. If you ask me," he whispered to Sally, "it was probably Peggy."

Sally laughed out of obligation. And out of relief.

She and Peter would be just fine. ⋆

Chapter 41

Friday, October 9, 1981
Long Beach, CA

The bell rang at Rogers Middle School, and passing period began. Jason saw Hank Knapick standing in front of his locker, planning not to let him pass. After a fair amount of teasing, Jason, still fresh off the pain of finding out last month that Augie had left for New York without saying goodbye, wouldn't sit still.

After all, he had come close to winning a radio contest and all the self-confidence that meant for a teen. With images of Dana (who had moved over the summer to Lawrence, Kansas, which nobody really knew about) and the disappointment of a new chapter that would not come, he turned and walked hurriedly to Hank. With a swift kick to the balls, resulting in Hank falling onto his right side in agony as the entirety of the eighth grade looked on, Jason Schneidman, who had dug for treasure at home plate at Dodger Stadium, instantly became a middle-school hero.

He walked home the usual way that day. East on Broadway about four blocks, then a sharp left through the alley just before St. Joseph. The blue gate was locked. He carefully reached over with his right arm so as not to snag his T-shirt on the jagged wood and let himself in. His mom was away for the weekend, and he felt the kind of freedom only a young man looking more forward than back could know.

The sun was just going down. Tomorrow, he would go skateboarding with Brandon at the UA movie theater on PCH. They would hide their boards in the sharp honeysuckle bushes just to the right of the exit door to Theater 3, where no one would ever look.

Management at the UA was aggressive in their enforcement of the no skateboard rule, and not wanting to miss the 2:50 matinee, Jason and Brandon could stomach the risk.

But before then, Jason had the entire night and house to himself. He drew open the living room curtain where the nascent sunset had begun to dim the Long Beach sky in all its hazy orange glory. He turned on the radio, perched on the bookshelf just below the Vonnegut section. The default was preset for 690 AM. But Jason reached (from a reclining position) his left arm up—which barely made it to the round silver dial—and switched the frequency to FM.

The station finder landed on KLAA, a new classic rock station that had launched months before.

Jason lay back fully as the resonant noise from the new rock station began to die down and become part of the landscape. And just before the sun finally dipped down over the Southern California skyline and the dark of night took hold on that Friday evening in the fall of 1981, he drifted off to sleep. ⋆

Epilogue

Early February 1996
Barstow, California
12:00pm

Fifteen years after the Mighty 690 had run a radio contest that would be baked into the fabric of suburban folklore forever, a woman in her sixties walked into a nondescript diner in Barstow, California, for a beer and a sit.

She had been traveling west on I-40 and needed the stop before barreling through to Santa Monica to see her mother. She had been asked to help after the stroke and knew her siblings and former father-in-law wouldn't do it.

As she settled into the third booth from the door and ordered, she caught her breath. On top of the napkin dispenser was yesterday's *Barstow Post*, stained from several coffee cups and at least one egg sandwich.

Flipping through the pages, waiting for her drink, she noticed the obituaries in the lower left corner of the third page. Passing the time and really in need of that beer, she read:

"Danny Baker, originally of Orange County, California, died yesterday of natural causes at his home in Barstow. He leaves no immediate family. Mr. Baker worked as a mechanic in the last few years of his life."

As the radio playing in the background switched from commercial to music, she looked up to see if the waitress was any closer to bringing her the drink. She wasn't. So she continued to read:

"For a brief period, Danny Baker was a professional motorcycle racer."

The waitress came to the table. Finally. The woman sipped her beer and listened to the radio.

★ ★ ★

Printed in the USA
CPSIA information can be obtained
at www.ICGtesting.com
LVHW071234270224
772932LV00021B/589

9 798989 467204